# THE SNAKE-MAN'S BANE

### HOWIE K. BENTLEY

### WILD HUNT BOOKS

# WILD HUNT BOOKS

Copyright © 2018 by Howie K. Bentley
All rights reserved

ISBN 978-1718653634

"All Will Be Righted on Samhain" originally appeared in *Swords of Steel*. Copyright Howie K. Bentley and David C. Smith, 2015
"The Heart of the Betrayer" originally appeared in *Swords of Steel II*. Copyright Howie K. Bentley, 2016
"…Where There Is No Sanctuary" originally appeared in *Cirsova Heroic Fantasy and Science Fiction Magazine* Issue #4 / Winter 2016. Copyright Howie K. Bentley, 2016
"Thannhausefeer's Guest" originally appeared in *Swords of Steel III*. Copyright Howie K. Bentley, 2017

All other stories are original to this publication and copyright to Howie K. Bentley.

Interior Layout by Black Heart Edits
    www.blackheartedits.com

Cover artwork by Lionel Baker II

Cover layout and digital editing by Jon Zaremba
    www.jonzaremba.com

Logo design by Louis Braquet

Printed in the United States of America

First Edition

www.howiebentley.com
www.amazon.com/author/howiebentley
howie@howiebentley.com

# Acknowledgements

Thanks to the following individuals: Jon Zaremba, D.M. Ritzlin, Alex Avdeev, David C. Smith, Andrea Dawn, Rich Smith, Morgan Holmes, Alex Kimball, Fletcher Vredenburgh, Lionel Baker II, and Louis Braquet.

## CONTENTS

The Snake-Man's Bane ............................................................. 1

All Will Be Righted on Samhain (with David C. Smith) ....................... 42

The Heart of the Betrayer ....................................................... 69

...Where There Is No Sanctuary ............................................... 97

Thannhausefeer's Guest ....................................................... 112

Full Moon Revenant ............................................................ 129

# THE SNAKE-MAN'S BANE

## CHAPTER I

## HEROO-THAAR

"I tell you, Hunthar. These streets ain't safe for you and me, let alone a pretty thing like her." Leric nodded toward the middle of the cobblestone road where two snake-men accosted a young lady clad in the white wedding gown and tall, miter-shaped headdress signifying her devotion to Nissis, the goddess of love. The reptilians were copper in color and had tails, though they walked upright on legs like a man and could wield weapons of steel with their arms. Clad in jewel-studded harnesses of leather and long silken breach clout, their mottled, naked limbs and torsos glistened in the blazing sun. The groom lay dazed on the ground with blood streaming from a gash beneath square-cut bangs down onto his light-blue wedding tunic. His wife screamed.

Moving lithely, one of the snake-men covered the woman's mouth with a scaled talon and grabbed her breast with his other, tearing her dress and exposing her alabaster flesh. Squeezing hard, he exhaled a sibilant chortle and blood trickled down the bride's snow-white nuptial gown. "Let's get this bitch inside. These old codgers don't need to see something that'll excite them too much!" The snake-man's forked tongue licked out, and his opened mouth showed curved fangs like ivory daggers.

Hunthar and Leric were far enough away that they barely could make out what the snake-men were saying, but they saw the reptilians look at them with oblique eyes peering out from under flattened heads. The two old men ducked into the doorway of a nearby tavern to avoid any malign intent that might come their way.

The snake-man clutching the struggling bride told his accomplice, "Get the groom. He can watch what we do to her."

They stopped when they heard a clopping of horse's hooves rounding the corner in front of the colonnade where they were engaged in their wickedness. A thin man with a sable, wide-brimmed hat shading his eyes ambled his night black stallion past the snake-men and their victims. Clad in a vulturine silk shirt, tights, and knee-high leather boots, man and steed seemed to meld together, save the visible half of the stranger's ghostly-white face framed by straight yellow hair nearly reaching his waist.

The snake-man gripping the groom released his quarry. The reptilian flicked his forked tongue and moved forward to command the newcomer to avert his gaze in conformity with recently established custom, but the rider didn't bother to look their way. The rider's hand gently brushed the hilt of the *seax* hanging at his right side, where the long knife was out of sight of slanted, serpentine eyes. Man and horse flowed on past the snake-men like a fleeting apparition dreamed up from Hel.

"Come on! Bring him!" the impatient snake-man hissed to his accomplice.

The second snake-man grabbed the groom by his short hair and dragged him. The two reptilians disappeared into the vacant building with their victims.

The rider sauntered his mount down the street and stopped in front of the tavern on the left end of the road. He raised his head, and icy blue eyes peered from under his hat up at the sign that read *The Proud Fools Inn*.

The man tethered his horse to the post in front of the tavern. He unfastened a large satchel from his saddle and slung it over his shoulder, entering The Proud Fools Inn as the setting sun blazed behind him like an ember in the cerulean sky.

"What'll it be, traveler?" the barkeep spoke. The big man wore a red tunic with gold bands on his arms. His greying hair was cropped short, as was the custom in Herod-Thaar.

"I'm Vegtam. I'm here to play tonight," the traveler said with a Nordic accent. He slung the satchel from his shoulder and laid it on the bar, opening it to show the barkeep the lute lying inside.

"Ah! The wandering minstrel. We don't get much entertainment down this way anymore since..."

"Well, in the lands to the north from which I hail, I'm called a Skald; but that's all right," Vegtam said.

"Well, by Nissis, I'm glad you came... and expect to be paid well for it, Vegtam!" The barkeep smiled.

"I do. That's why I'm here," replied the Skald.

"Sargas. Sargas Tuun. Owner of the The Proud Fools."

"Sargas, I need to find shelter for my mount, get a room, and sleep a while before I play."

Sargas Tuun shouted, and a boy came from the back. "Tithus, show Vegtam a stall in the stable where he can keep his horse while he's staying with us, then show him his room."

Once the horse was stabled and provided water and nourishment, and the boy had shown Vegtam his room, the Skald returned to the bar.

"Drink?" Sargas asked.

"Do you have arrack?" Vegtam replied.

"You're just in luck!" Sargas said, half turning and pointing to an ornate sapphire amphora on a shelf behind him. "Just got a shipment from the Far East yesterday."

"I'll have a little before I bed down. I'll be drinking quite a bit more when I wake up for the night. I have the contract your employee delivered to me some weeks ago. You still agree that drinks are in addition to the fee for my performance, correct?"

Sargas nodded soberly, knowing well the stories about how much Gurmanians could imbibe.

"Good." Vegtam took the crudely fashioned cup of arrack and looked at the two old men seated at the table across from him in ardent conversation. *I wonder what these two old bastards are worrying about. Seems like a good opportunity to catch up on the news in Herod-Thaar.*

Vegtam walked over to the table closest to theirs and sat, sipping sparingly at his cup while listening to the conversation between the two greybeards.

"Leric, there's nothing to be done, aside from fleeing this accursed land. We thought the stories about the snake-men were tales told by the fey—by those who saw devils and goblins everywhere they looked, like something out of the ruins of Nephasth."

Leric, a short, portly fellow who was bald on top of his head, quaffed his ale and nodded. "Well, all the time the snake-men were operating in secret, throwing the Mosuuls at us, stirring up war between them and us; and Emperor Granlamb was all too happy to take the conquered from their decimated lands, knowing good and well they were too damned barbaric to assimilate!"

Hunthar nodded, his kind eyes set back in a long somber face and his drooping mustache making him look like a hound dog. "And knowing that'd be the end of us, which is what they want."

Leric nervously pushed his drinking jack around. "It weren't bad enough that those swarthy Mosuulian devils moved in and outraged our women, but the monarchy looked the other way, said nothing was happening. The priests of Hewahay even said it was imminent that the dusky devils breed with our women. Our own men have been losing their heads to Granlamb's executioners for defending their wives and daughters…"

"We are told we can't even defend ourselves," Hunthar interposed. "Now the snake-men are making it known they covet our women, as well, knowing we can't do anything about it. The Mosuulian refugees were the first step, setting up for the snake-men to come in and start breeding the women. Their goal is to set their spawn upon all the thrones of the kingdoms of man. And Herod-Thaar is now their base."

Vegtam tightened his lips and squinted his eyes, ruminating over the news the two greybeards were unknowingly providing him.

"And what of Granlamb's henchman, Count Amschauld? I don't doubt that he's a shape-changer himself. Half man and half snake-man," Leric said.

"Aye. So it is said," Hunthar replied. "Granlamb himself is but a puppet controlled by the snake-men. They're all nothing but predators who destroy everything in their paths. They use us in their connivances and call us 'useless eaters'. That is why I am telling you, if you expect to live much longer—at least a dignified and painless existence—you'd better make for the border of Thorkistani where the lands aren't plagued by desert savages, shape-shifting sub-humans, and snake-men."

"Aye. Draco Kharn rules all of Thorkistani with an iron fist," Leric said.

"Not even the snake-men will go there after they have seen how he's beaten back the Mosuuls and the cruelties he's heaped on their swarthy hides, impaled on spears in front of his castle while he looks at them and drinks their chieftains' blood from their own skulls," Hunthar said.

"For now, anyway," Leric said. "They have their hands full ruining everything here. But I fear it's a little late to escape Herod-Thaar."

Hunthar shook his head. "My great grandsire, Siegfried Kalmbach, served in the campaign to take the land back from the Mosuul long ago. He brought his family and stayed here. Our people shouldn't be in lands where the desert sun burns so hot. It's baked the native's brains. It's always been this way. They're blood-drunk from the heat and crazy from worshipping Illyahay, the god of torment and death—the same deity worshipped by the snake-men. The monarchy and snake-men call him Hewahay, but he's the same sandy god."

"Lower your voice!" Leric said in a forceful whisper. "Do you want to be hauled away and put to death? I heard that merely a touch from them is venomous, and their victims lie and rot, suffering for weeks before they die."

Vegtam focused intently to hear all of their conversation.

Continuing in a whisper, Hunthar said, "I'm off on the morrow for the border of Thorkistani… or death."

"You are drunk!" Leric snarled back at him. "The whole border of Herod-Thaar is heavily guarded! How do you intend to cross it? And what do you get for fleeing south? More snake-men! The monarchy has the border to Thorkistani heavily guarded by their soldiers. If you're caught, you go before the tribune; then you lie on a nice comfortable divan and rot while venom courses through your bulging veins. The only way out of here and clear to the border of Thorkistani is through the ruins of Nephasth, and you know good and well what they say about that place!"

"What?! That it's haunted by a sorcerer? Xexor-Wroth? A red devil with horns, from stories to frighten unruly children!" Hunthar snapped.

"So were the snake-men… a few years back," said Leric.

Hunthar looked dolefully down in defeat at his near-empty flagon of ale and echoed his friend's words, "So were the snake-men."

Vegtam had heard enough. He had to play tonight and needed to sleep. He got up and traversed the steps to his room at the top of the stairs.

## CHAPTER II

## LOST IN A SONG

Flames licked in copper cressets mounted on poles, casting uneven shadows across the darkened room. The patrons of The Proud Fools Inn sat in silence as Vegtam's lithe fingers floated across the lute strings like feathers, pulling at the heartstrings of men and women alike. The piece was a minor key affair, an old Skaldavian ballad that told of love lost and never realized until the death of a lover. Vegtam's voice was a rich, sonorous baritone until it climbed up in pitch to a crescendo and he left off singing and went into an instrumental improvisation on the lute. His note choices formed a melody from exotic scales sending shivers up his listeners' spines. The sequenced scalar passages became faster and faster. His fingers blurred as he ascended the neck of his lute with diminished arpeggios that segued back into his high head voice, returning to a chorus that brought tears to the eyes of all within hearing.

Sometimes his own performances reminded him of fleeting faces in the night—women he had known; most, however, briefly. Though his memories of them faded as he moved from town to town always in search of better pay, the short-lived affairs often framed her—whoever she might be on a particular night—into the one he couldn't forget.

He reached for the battered stone chalice and drank deeply of the heady attack. He couldn't expect his listeners to be moved by the music unless he moved himself, and the more he drank the more moved was he. *One more drink before the next song.*

"Any requests?" Vegtam called out to the packed inn.

A drunken soldier shouted for an idiotic sing-along. Vegtam smiled and adjusted one of the tuning keys on his lute before launching into the bawdy tune. He would start singing, then drop out and just pluck his lute as the audience picked up the song and carried it on their own.

Two lovelies, scantily clad in brightly colored silken garments barely covering their breasts and groins appeared in front of Vegtam. They whirled and pirouetted to the wild sing-along. One of them was thin with flaming red hair, and the other raven-haired, with curves in all of the right places. Vegtam caught a glimpse of wild blue eyes set back in her piquant face as she tossed her sable tresses and her ample bosom jiggled.

*She's the one I'll be bedding tonight!*

When he ended the song, his listeners burst into applause. The hooting and screaming carried out into the night air. He grinned into his cup and quaffed deeply.

He thought about the conversation between the two old men, Hunthar and Leric, and he reflected on the unfortunate couple and their reptilian oppressors he had seen upon entering Herod-Thaar.

*Time to change it up a little. Something in a minor key again, but this time without the melancholia. No, this one should be dramatic as the vengeance of an Æsir god.*

The faces in the crowded inn were like jack-o-lanterns glowing in the dimly-lit room, and the arrack sent his muse soaring on wings of dark fantasia. He remembered bits of a song a strange one-eyed guest had sung on a stormy night when he was a child. The singer's name had been Vegtam, just like his own.

He slowly sipped the arrack and tuned his lute again, giving himself time to think about how the words went before launching into the only recently-remembered song. What he didn't remember, he would improvise. That is what a Skald of his renown did.

A smile spread across Vegtam's face and he played a galloping rhythm in twelve-eight time. When he had repeated the opening motif twice, he started singing:

*Oh, the Wild Hunt rides by tonight.*
*Father One-Eye looks for a fight.*
*The sons of man should stay inside.*
*Sleipnir snorts, head thrown back in pride.*

*Death stalks the woods and rides the wind.*
*A curse upon the sons of men,*
*For those who witness Odin's hunt*
*He shall be split from back to front,*
*Hung upside down, bled like a boar,*
*Feasted upon by goats of Thor.*

The dark-haired beauty spun and pirouetted, stopped in front of him and boldly drank from Vegtam's cup. Her wild eyes met his gaze, and she turned to the audience of The Proud Fools as Vegtam launched into another verse.

*The gods of Asgard scourge the Earth,*
*Reset man for winter's rebirth,*
*Destroying monsters and frost giants,*
*Killing snake-men in defiance...*

Vegtam didn't know if the last line came from the heady liquor's ability to dull his memory and cause him to start improvising words early in the song or if it was his present milieu and a desire to give the occupants of The Proud Fools some joy and hope in their inebriation.

As Vegtam sang the last line he noticed a figure surrounded by armed men in jupon and chainmail enter the inn and make his way to the center of the room. Men and women seated at the tables nearby got up and left. Little grey hair covered the sides of the newcomer's head, and beneath the man's pate protruded a prodigious nose that seemed to suck his two beady eyes close together. The man's jaw was firmly set, and he fixed his cruel gaze on Vegtam. The newcomer was clad in a purple robe of samite.

Sargas Tuun stood a distance behind the man, eyes wide in horror, gesturing for Vegtam to stop singing. Vegtam saw the innkeeper and called on the reserves of his virtuosity to finish the song as an instrumental.

With a cue from Sargas Tuun, the dancing girls stopped. No one applauded. The tension was paramount. All Vegtam could hear was the creaking of tables, chairs, and the floorboards of the inn as over half of his audience cleared the establishment.

The newcomer raised his voice in mock protest to Vegtam and the patrons still left in the room, "Oh, please do continue."

Obviously, here was a nobleman with some affiliation to the monarchy or snake-men that Hunthar and Leric had spoken of, but Vegtam was by now too drunk to care. With a shrug of his shoulders, he emptied his cup and swept his gaze around the room at the others who were either inebriated like him or just proud fools. The room filled up with Vegtam's sonorous voice, and his hand struck a rasgueado on the lute. Another bawdy number and the remnants of the room came alive again, though the dancing girls had already made themselves scarce and did not return.

## CHAPTER III

## A LIFE OF CRIME

Vegtam awoke to the sound of birds chirping and shallow breathing behind him. A hint of dawn peaked through the shutters over the window across from his bed. He looked down and could see her arm and raven locks draped over his side.

I think her name was Tawna.

He didn't remember much of the latter half of the night, but she might have been good enough that he would want to bed her again a few times before leaving Herod-Thaar.

Vegtam moved slightly. She wrapped her arm around him and broke the silence. "How was last night?"

"I don't know," he said. "I was drunk. Maybe you can tell me."

"Not bad for a drunk," she replied. "What are you doing in this accursed land? I thought minstrels latched onto wealthy patrons and lived a life of comfort and certitude inside castle walls."

"A life of *servitude* is more like it. I'm my own man and go where I please. My reputation as a musician has grown to the point that innkeepers from afar have heard of me and will pay good coin for me to sing to their customers," Vegtam said.

"Besides, I figured it was time for a little sojourn in the eastern sectors. There was a disagreement between myself and a nobleman in I'Latillia that ended with my dagger in his gut. A warlord named Argantyr has risen to power, and it won't be long before he has toppled the throne of I'Latillia. He comes from Tuatha and already rules most of Skaldavia. They call him Fenris there—the Wolf King. Once the Odoacer Dynasty has fallen, it will be safe for me to return to roam where I may.

"I might ask the same of you, dear girl. What do you do in these troubled lands?"

"My father was a merchant from the city of Laguna in V'risia. We traveled with the caravans back and forth between Laguna and the eastern sectors. My mother died when I was young. Father's health eventually declined until he could no longer stand the arduous journeys over leagues of desert sands. He made our home in Herod-Thaar, and we lived a dull but peaceful existence until they started showing themselves," Tawna said.

"The snake-men?"

"Aye," she whispered. "I am loath to even speak of them for fear one shall appear."

"What of your father?" asked Vegtam.

"He died eight years ago. His heart was weak, and I never thought these arid lands were best for his condition. He left me with enough coin for a moderate existence. Sargas Tuun pays me to help him run The Proud Fools. I can use the extra money. Since they—the snake-men—have come into Herod-Thaar, the monarchy keeps raising taxes. The dancing I mostly do for excitement. There is so little of it here."

"Why did you leave when that man came in last night?" Vegtam asked.

She drew in a deep breath and exhaled, whispering excitedly, "That was Count Amschauld. He is Emperor Granlamb's right-hand man, if man he be. Some say he is a shapeshifter, and he's been seen in the company of the snake-men on more than one occasion. It is said that when he sets his eyes on a woman or child that person goes missing, never to be seen again."

"Why do you not leave these monster-infested lands, Tawna?"

"I have no living relatives back in V'risia. Life in Herod-Thaar is all I have known, and even if I wanted to go, I hear the monarchs have closed the borders to Thorkistani since the snake-men have come. No one is to leave."

Vegtam nodded. "I had no problem getting in. But I don't plan on staying long. The pay is good, but it is too hot here for one of the Nord blood such as myself."

She moaned as he gently slipped from her side and sat up on the edge of the bed.

"Where are you going? I thought musicians slept in the day."

"I need a drink of water. My blood is mostly arrack by now."

"All you wanted was strong drink last night, so that's all I brought to your room. If you want water it's downstairs in the back."

Vegtam arose from the bed and slipped on his silk shirt and tights and put on his boots. The inn was silent save for the creaking steps as he made his way down to Sargas's kitchen to find water.

The Skald poured the water from the amphora into a large stone cup he found and drained the contents. He tilted his head back, pouring another cupful onto his head, and rubbed it into his face. He found a towel and began drying himself when he heard a woman's scream come from upstairs.

"Tawna?!" he growled.

Vegtam crept furtively up the stairs. He could hear a man's muffled voice and the sounds of struggling issuing from his room. No other sound could be heard about the tavern.

"Why did you run away last night, tavern wench? Where is your paramour now? Aye?" the man shouted and there was a loud slapping sound. Tawna cried out.

The Skald drew the slim dagger from the hidden sheath inside his boot and kicked the door open. Before him stood the man who had driven away most of his audience last night: Count Amschauld. The Count was accompanied by a snake-man.

Vegtam lunged to meet the snake-man. The reptilian turned to counter Vegtam, but Vegtam leapt on the bed and back off onto the snake-man. Both man and monster crashed to the floor. The snake-man bared his fangs, and his forked tongue flicked out his mouth; Vegtam quickly thrust his dagger up through the underside of the reptilian's mouth and drove it into the snake-man's head.

Count Amschauld turned loose of Tawna, and his sword hissed free of its scabbard. He slashed at Vegtam's head. Vegtam backed up and grabbed his lute from where it leaned in a corner of the room. Amschauld slashed again with his sword, and Vegtam ducked. Quickly, Vegtam moved in and crashed his lute down onto the side of Amschauld's head with a resounding crack and a jangling of strings as the instrument shattered and flew to pieces. Count Amschauld sank to the floor and lay still.

Tawna was breathing hard but appeared uninjured. Vegtam found his belt and the long knife sheathed there. He squatted and pressed the blade on the writhing snake-man's neck. Straining, he cut the monster's throat. Green ichor jetted forth as the reptilian continued to writhe on the floor in its death throes.

Vegtam placed his foot on the snake-man's head to hold it down as he retrieved his dagger.

"Come on, Vegtam. This way! You must leave now. Make haste!" a voice called from the doorway. It was Sargas Tuun. "You must go too, Tawna. It's no longer safe for you in Herod-Thaar."

Vegtam and Tawna followed Sargas Tuun quickly down the spiral stairway.

"In here!" Sargas said.

They followed Sargas into the kitchen where he slid back a shelf. There lay a large rug. He removed the rug, revealing a trapdoor. Vegtam helped Sargas lift the door, and Sargas addressed him: "Down the ladder. Go about one hundred feet. There you will meet a wall. Go right and you will start seeing light. The further you go, the brighter it gets. This will take you out of a small cave mouth in an embankment behind the barn where your horse is stabled. I've already sent Tithus to saddle your horse, and there will be a roan in the adjacent stall for Tawna. Leave by the gate in the western wall. It's a small portal, but always open. So confident are the snake-men that their rule is absolute; they don't even bother to guard that one. Head west and ride for the border of Thorkastani. It is a longshot, but you can't stay here."

"And what of you, Sargas?" Tawna asked. "A snake-man was killed in your inn."

"There will be questions, but Vegtam knocked out that son of a bitch Count Amschauld before he saw me. Hopefully, he will just lie there and die, but I doubt it. I didn't know your lute was that hard, Vegtam."

Vegtam smiled wryly and nodded his head before climbing down the ladder. "I did. I've tested it on a few heads before. It was time for a new one anyway. You had better go before Amschauld regains consciousness and summons soldiers, Sargas," he called up from the cellar as he and Tawna vanished into the darkness.

---

The hooves of Vegtam's steed struck sparks off the flinty road as they exited the city and raced for the hills beyond. Tawna's roan galloped quickly alongside Vegtam's mount. A trumpet sounded in the distance.

"That means the main gate is open and they are now chasing us!" Tawna cried out over the rumble of horses' hooves.

"This isn't the first time for me!" Vegtam shouted. "You said you wanted some excitement in your life, woman! Welcome to a life of crime!"

On and on the two fugitives raced past orchards of pomegranate and apricot and the fields of sesame surrounding and lying beyond the city, driving their mounts as hard as they would go. It seemed like an eternity had passed, though Vegtam knew it could not have been nearly an hour since they fled Herod-Thaar.

As they passed the blackened mouth of a pass, Tawna reined in her horse and called to Vegtam. Vegtam brought the night-black stallion to a stop and galloped back to where Tawna sat her mount. Turning, he saw dust clouds boiling up in the distance. It would take a sizeable host of mounted men to kick up that kind of fuss.

Tawna pointed to the mouth of the pass and cried out frantically, "Through there! Just a few miles and we enter Nephasth. They say it is inhabited by the old sorcerer, Xexor-Wroth, and the devils he calls up. Even the snake-men won't go there.

"When I was a little girl I was playing and ranged far from home. They found me near here. I remember the entrance to that pass. My father was frightened for me, and I didn't understand why. I have always thought it foolish superstition. Now, I don't know. There may be something there, but right now it is our only hope of escaping."

Vegtam nodded his head and said, "Better a devil that has yet to show itself than what is closing in on us. Lead the way."

Tawna dug her heels into her roan's ribs and set off at a gallop.

Vegtam's black stallion raced behind her.

Through the gorge the horses thundered and galloped, across ledges and around crags. Their steeds plunged down the narrow pathway winding to the valley below. They slowed their mounts as they entered a narrow gorge with high basalt walls jutting up to the open sky. The tapered path finally debouched into the low-lying verdurous dale. The sun was setting when they rode onto the floor of the valley of Nephasth.

## CHAPTER IV

## XEXOR-WROTH

The darkly-tarnished bronze door slammed shut like the sealing of a massive tomb behind a hooded figure clad in a voluminous robe of crimson. The figure entered the chamber and shuffled about in the subterranean depths of the dimly-lit corridor. Stopping before a brazier upborne on a tall pedestal, he held a bony hand that ended in long black fingernails over the apparatus. The hand looked more like a wyvern's claw than something belonging to a creature that should walk upright like a man. Bloodlike flames burst forth from the brazier and showed tables covered in curious bottles and various configurations of glass tubes woven together in complex serpentine patterns. Moldering tomes filled with gramarye lined the shelves along the walls. *Diabolus Occulta Ahrimanios*, *The Black Book of Narathkor*, *A Treatise On the Transformation of Man to Beast*, and *Pacts With Those Who Cometh Forth by Night* were there amongst countless others.

The hooded figure picked up a sturdy ebon box with ease and set it down on a high stone slab. He unfastened the latches holding the box shut and with a loud jangling poured a pile of bones onto the slab. A skull rolled out on top, leering up at him.

The robed figure addressed the pile of bones in a sepulchral rasp, "Oh, Valhia! How many years has it been? I don't know. The ages seem but a season past. And I have followed your incarnations in dark Vysperias's waters that flow under our abode and show me past, present, and future—if only but for a moment's time. Once you were a great white queen in the black jungles of Tarthiqqua, but I didn't recognize you until it was too late and you were dying. And once you were a butterfly, dying even as I set eyes upon you, and then but a drop of rain that was gone as soon as it fell. Aeons have passed, and I look into the waters for you each day; but I only see my own face withered and infested by the demons I have summoned down through the ages. Once, you knew me as a man. Could you bear to look upon me now? Xexor-Wroth, who was once the man you loved, who is still the mightiest of necromancers, but who is powerless to bring back his lost Valhia!"

The sorcerer laughed bitterly. "I could have brought your body back long ago. But your Ka? Your Sheut? Your Ren, Ba, and Ib? They scattered like dust in a storm and fled their dark pursuers when you breathed your last breath.

"I have lain with many a corpse raised up from the House of Shades since I lost you, but all pales in comparison to my Valhia. I would not have you walk about languidly and your cold body lie soulless alongside me in our bed."

Xexor-Wroth turned away from the pile of bones and fell silent for some time. Then, he turned back around and resumed speaking. "But I have looked into the water and I have seen the Key to the Rune Realms draw nigh. Aye! What we once thought was legendry is out there, and there is one nearby who holds it. I have just dispatched the Aklo to seize the Key and return it to me.

"In life, there was none fairer than Valhia, the Witch of Nephasth. Much has changed since we parted. We freely delved deep into the darkest of magicks and summoned defined presences to do our will. We made pact after pact with the demons. We were powerful then, and even now there is no magician more powerful than Xexor-Wroth! I watched the demons rot you away on the inside, and even then you were beautiful in death. I kept calling on them, thinking you died because you were weak. But they have fed on me in a different way."

He pulled his hood back and revealed a face covered in transparent skin with a faintly rubrous tint. Had dead Valhia's skull still possessed the faculties of sight, she would have seen the blood flowing through the clearly visible veins in Xexor-Wroth's face and the short, once white, now yellowing horns that protruded from each side of the top of his head. She would have seen the dark hollows that were once eye sockets and the burning amber lights that were once the eyes of a human sorcerer.

"I have merely to speak of that which will be, and it is; yet I pay a price. The energies that I command in turn feed on me. If only we had known this in past ages. The true key to mastery isn't in defined energies. It is in the invocation of defining energies that allow one to create... create servitors, as I have created the Aklo, but also create demons and even create gods and the worlds they inhabit. All of this is possible with the Runes."

Xexor-Wroth stretched his claw-like hand to a nearby bookshelf and took from it a slender tome bound in the hide of a serpent. The only writing on the book was a series of bind-runes spanning the length of the spine.

He gripped the book with both bony hands and held it up for the skull and bones of Valhia to see, as if something of his former leman still haunted her pitiful remains.

"*Far Beyond Egregorian Shadows!* Some of the fragments contained herein were written down in an eldritch eighteen-rune row of which little is told elsewhere. It took me years to translate some of the more difficult passages, but finally I am confident I possess the knowledge to rid myself of these parasites and restore myself to a man and you to the woman you were in the prime of your life."

The pulsing yellow lights that were once eyes beamed from Xexor-Wroth's head, and he stretched the transparent sheen that served as his skin into a sickening rictus. "I have the book, but that is only half of the equation. Even now, a man rides this way—a priest of Odin—whom the waters of Vysperia reveal to be the keeper of the Key to the Rune Realms. At first they showed me but a shadow riding forth from the mists, but as he draws nigh I see him clearer and clearer."

Xexor-Wroth turned to a pool formed of porphyry protruding from the floor, wherein stood the waters of Vysperia. The warlock waved his hands, making complex gestures above the large igneous formation and sonorously intoned: "Waters of Vysperia that runneth from the deepest depths of time and space, wherein the Great Winged Wyrm gnaweth the roots of the world until such time as it is no more, show me the Key to the Rune Realms. Baal-Pteor! Amon! Marbas! Astaroth!"

The still waters showed the horned head and demonic face of Xexor-Wroth to himself. Anon, the Vysperia waters briefly shimmered and bubbled. Then, they became still again and showed him the image of a mailed warrior in a horned helmet and cloak of blue riding a great white stallion. The man wore an eyepatch, but his good eye gleamed a cruel blue light that burned like the blazing sun down on the icy Nordlands beneath a shock of long grey hair.

Xexor-Wroth had his back turned on the skull and bones of Valhia, but still he addressed his long-dead leman. "The priest of Odin himself rides into the valley of Nephasth even now." The warlock raised his voice. "Nephasth, my kingdom! Nephasth, my tomb! I have told you I can't leave here for fear the demons possessing me, and bracing my immortality will abandon me and I will fall to dust. But by my gramarye I have brought him here, and I will have the Key!"

The sorcerer waved his hands in the air making another gesture, and the scene in the waters shifted to four large black shapes with bat-like wings gliding over the verdant valley of Nephasth in the setting sun. The shapes converged and wheeled high above like vultures circling carrion.

## CHAPTER V

## PRIEST OF ODIN

Sitting by a babbling brook, Tawna splashed cool clean water over her face while Vegtam checked to make sure their mounts were securely tethered to the date trees nearby. Vegtam lay down and put his ear to the ground. Tawna looked at him inquisitively. Vegtam raised his head and shook it.

"No. It seems we have lost them for now," Vegtam said. He went over by Tawna and filled an empty wine flask with water. "Just in case…"

A rustle of leathern wings sounded nearby, and Vegtam and Tawna caught sight of black shapes descending amid the trees beyond. The shapes were too large to be birds. Vegtam held up his hand to silence Tawna, then gestured for her to follow him.

They lit out on foot, walking softly towards the copse of trees where they had seen the things land. Vegtam could hear a man shouting in Nordic. He understood the words since the man's language was akin to his native Gurmanian.

"By Gungnir! Come forth ye wicked! Tonight you'll dine in Niflheim with all the other devils of your accursed race!" the man bellowed. A horrible cacophony of screeches answered.

Coming upon the thicket, Vegtam and Tawna knelt behind two large acacias and peered into the verdant clearing ahead. An armored man sat his rearing horse and slashed his hefty broadsword at two winged demons swooping down on him. One horned devil lay on its back, transfixed by a spear and convulsing, its wings beating the ground in its death throes. Another lay still on the earth, prone, with its head several feet from its shiny black body.

The two remaining monsters swooped back and forth, circling the warrior. The things emitted obscene, blood-curdling screeches.

The man turned his steed to face one demon and slashed back-handed at the creature sailing in behind him. His horse reared again. One piercing blue eye looked out from under the man's horned helmet; the other was covered with an eyepatch. His dark blue cloak was slung back revealing his rent chainmail and blood flowing from myriad wounds. He turned his horse yet again as the winged demons continued their relentless onslaught.

"We must do something to help him," Tawna whispered to Vegtam.

Vegtam nodded his head and slipped the slim dagger from his boot that had earlier that day ended the life of a snake-man. He leapt to his feet, and with a flash of his arm the dagger licked out and struck the black devil in the back of the neck between the base of its head and the top of its knobby spine. The creature's wings fluttered, and it faltered.

At that moment the man raced forth on his steed and slammed his blade upward into the things breastbone. Momentarily, the warrior's sword was stuck in the abomination, and that was enough time for the other demon to alight on the man from behind as the warrior wrenched his sword free. He fell from his horse, losing his grip on the sword hilt. The horned helm toppled from his head onto the verdurous floor of the clearing along with man and winged devil.

The demon had the man's arms pinioned but a moment, then it held his head in its unnaturally large talons, digging its thick, elongated nails into his head. Blood seeped out over the man's face. No sooner had the creature let go of the warrior's arms and moved its claws to his head than a long dagger flashed in the man's hand, and he drove the blade repeatedly into the thing's back. But the demon continued to hang on. Veins bulged in the warrior's forehead.

Vegtam drew the *seax* from the sheath at his waist and motioned for Tawna to stay put. He raced across the clearing like a tiger. Leaping onto the thing's back and locking his legs tightly around its torso, he grabbed it by one horn and pulled its head back, slicing the demon's throat. A thick, oily substance slowly seeped from the opening. Vegtam saw the demon had four ebon eyes forming a diamond shape in the center of its forehead, a snout like a pig, and a mouthful of saw-like teeth from which it now gurgled a horrid cry. The warrior on the ground drove his dagger into the creature's chest and shouted, "Quick! My sword! Strike off its head!"

Vegtam frantically clutched at the warrior's sword where it lay on the ground, and raising it, two-handed, hacked at the thing's neck. The third blow severed head from torso, and the thing flopped around like a hellish chicken and lay still.

Blood covered the warrior's bearded face, and he labored to breathe. Vegtam said, "Hold on, and I will get water."

The warrior managed to raise a hand and gasped, "No… no time. I must tell you." Though the wizened warrior was dying, his one blue eye smoldered like a burning star upon Vegtam.

"You," the warrior gasped, "are the one. It is by no accident you came… upon me as I battled the sorcerer's servitors, and… now I lie here awaiting death. Oh, I will feast and drink with Odin in his great hall tonight, but you now have a heavy weight on your shoulders, Skald. Such have the Norns woven your wyrd." The old man weakly chuckled.

"And you wonder how I know you are a Skald? He tells me… tells me even now, standing in his golden armor beyond…" The dying warrior raised his hand and languidly pointed to the sky. "You have heard Odin himself sing his rune songs… and they are in you, just as his blood is in you. Think you… he only fathered gods such as Thor, Baldur, Tyr, Heimdall… and Bragi?" the greybeard choked out. "Many are the sons of Odin; some… some of them born to mortal women."

Vegtam spoke, "I never knew my father, but I remember…"

But the dying warrior held up his hand to silence Vegtam. "All will be revealed in time, but now I must tell you…" the warrior struggled harder to talk as he gasped for air. "There is a sorcerer in the Valley of Nephasth. His flesh is infested by demons, and his mind and body twisted into a devil himself. He is aeons old because the… the demons hold him up… keep him alive. He dares not venture far from his devil-haunted abode… for fear they will abandon him and… and he will crumble to naught.

"It is his desire to invade the very realms of creation: the Rune Realms. I have ridden far from the rim of Skaldavia, near the borders where dwell the Æsir. The warlock… thinks his spells summon me so that he may steal the Key to the Rune Realms, but I have… have ridden forth of my own accord. For even without the Key I possess, there are others, well-hidden though they may be… who also possess other keys… to enter.

"Time is on the warlock's side, for the demons who serve him… won't let him die as long as they… hang onto him like leeches… and eventually his magick will reach out for another, possibly… weaker guardian. I had come to slay him, but I must pass this burden on to you, Skald; for like me… I see in you the Æsir blood, and you must complete what I set out to do."

The dying warrior was gasping hard for breath now. "Follow… follow the setting sun into the ruins of Nephasth. The warlock will show himself. Listen… listen carefully to me. You must take the Key to the Rune Realms and hold it while you say, 'A third song I know, which is good to me, for a fetter to my enemies. I dull the steel of my foes, so that their swords will cut no more.' Then, chant : 'Th-Th-Thorn', until the rune manifests. The protector of the Rune Realms will show itself… himself. Tell him what is afoot… and your work will be done."

"It sounds easy enough," Vegtam said.

"It won't be." The old man coughed, and Vegtam could see blood inside the warrior's mouth.

The dying warrior raised his hand and tore his eyepatch away. Where his eye had once been, kaleidoscopic swirls stirred in iridescent splendor. Looking upon the thing made Vegtam drunk. The warrior plucked the object from his eye socket and the colors were snuffed out like a candle flame blown out in the wind. The old man placed the thing inside Vegtam's hand, and with a firm grip that was surprising for a dying man he closed Vegtam's hand tightly into a fist around the object.

"The Key to the Rune Realms…. The Valkyries come now…" the old man said, and his head fell back. He lay there motionless with his empty eye socket uncovered and one good eye staring into the infinity that was death.

Vegtam looked over his shoulder at Tawna and shook his head. He closed the dead warrior's eye and stood up, looking down at his own still-clenched fist. He opened his hand and saw a milky, opaque crystal cut at irregular angles. Vegtam turned the object over in his hand, counting the sides of the thing. There were eighteen uneven sides, each engraved with a blood-red rune.

Vegtam and Tawna stood in the clearing a little way from where the warrior had died. A sudden rustle of wings, and Vegtam and Tawna thought more of the winged demons had come for them. They whirled and looked about, but nothing was there. When they looked in the direction of the warrior's corpse, it was gone.

"The Valkyries," Vegtam mumbled. "The Valkyries.

"Best to rest now, and be on our way for the border of Thorkistani tomorrow."

## CHAPTER VI

## MEMORIES OF A STRANGE GUEST

The moon shone brightly on the glade where they were encamped. An open fire crackled and spit sparks as Vegtam and Tawna sat in silence, eating dried meat and figs Vegtam had taken from his saddlebag.

"Do you not think it wise to follow the warrior-priest's directions?" Tawna asked.

"I'm not sure what to think," Vegtam answered.

"Maybe this talisman can help us escape to Thorkistani," she said.

"Maybe." Vegtam furrowed his brow and after a moment of silence he said, "I never knew my father. My mother was a witch. I am not entirely unfamiliar with denizens of the netherworld as she used to entertain strange guests from time to time. One of them was a man named Vegtam— his name like mine. I think she named me after him.

"I remember one night when all the people were afraid to go outside. I couldn't have been more than ten years old. The locals whispered of the Wild Hunt, and the sky split with lightning; thunder roared so loudly it shook our dwelling.

"There was a knocking at the door. My mother opened it, and there he stood. He was tall and filled the doorway. He had one eye and wore a hat like this one." Vegtam took the black, wide-brimmed hat from his head

## THE SNAKE-MAN'S BANE

and gently brushed his fingers over it.

"She greeted him as an old friend, and they exchanged pleasantries. He told her he had journeyed far. I listened, enraptured, as he told tales of ice giants and runes, magick weapons, and a ship that sailed over land and sea. Then he noticed the lute my mother had hanging on the wall and took it down. He quickly tuned it and started playing. He sang a song. It was about the Runes, and there were eighteen strophes.

"'A third song I know, which is good to me, for a fetter to my enemies. I dull the steel of my foes, so that their swords will cut no more.' That is what the Odin priest told me to chant. It was the third strophe of the song old Vegtam sung that night. I don't know how, but after that night I picked up the lute and it wasn't long before I'd mastered it. I'd never tried to play before other than flailing at the open strings to annoy those nearby. There was something magickal about that night."

"What do you think it means?"

"I am still trying to make sense of it. The old warrior talked of the Runes and the Sons of Odin as he lay dying. He told me that Odin's rune songs are in me, just as his blood is. I don't know how he knew I was a Skald, but he knew. And he told me I was of the blood of the Æsir, like himself. I am not sure what it all means, but as you said, maybe this talisman can help us reach Thorkistani safely." He turned the crystal over in his hand, touching each rune with his fingers.

"Though the moon is full and would illumine our way, I think we should bed down in this grove and rest. We'll be on our way tomorrow."

Vegtam placed the crystal in a pouch that hung at his belt. He figured it was better to keep it as close to him as possible at all times. He took two blankets from his horse and threw one on the ground, motioning for Tawna to join him. They laid down on the blanket together, and Vegtam draped the second blanket over them. It wasn't long before they both were asleep.

---

Vegtam's eyes sprang open. The earth about them rumbled. The ground exploded and dirt and rocks shot into the air as nearby trees were uprooted and fell over. Vegtam and Tawna leapt to their feet and Vegtam shouted, "Quickly! The horses!" Before they could make it to the other side of the clearing where their mounts were tethered, a hellish shape burst from the Earth and showed itself in the light of the full moon.

The giant scorpion looked as though it were formed of enormous chunks of ruby. Its eyes were amber flames blazing in a head joined to a long body. The colossus had claws that snapped on either side of the creature. It reared up on four pairs of legs and lashed its segmented tail.

Vegtam whipped the dagger from his boot and threw it into the thing's jeweled underbelly. The blade stuck there, and the monstrosity showed its rage by rubbing its front legs together. The result of the monster's stridulation resulted in a horrible cacophony of dissonance like a hellish pit full of stringed instruments playing out of tune.

Vegtam and Tawna covered their ears, but the awful sound drove them to their knees. Vegtam remembered the crystal talisman and fought against the paralysis-inducing pandemonium that pressed him to the ground. Finally, his hand touched the pouch and his fingers worked frantically to unfasten the strings. But the giant, jeweled scorpion's tail whipped around and lashed down on Vegtam's back. The Skald fell limp on the sward, the crystal talisman falling from the opened pouch and rolling in the darkness of a shadowy copse. Across from Vegtam, Tawna lay prone on the ground with her hands over her head. The scorpion paced over to Vegtam and scooped him up in one of its claws. It then turned in a westerly direction and scuttled rapidly forward.

---

Xexor-Wroth's cachinnations rang throughout the subterranean chamber as he strained to see into the darkness of night while the colossal scorpion raised aloft its claw and carried Vegtam's limp body like a prize it had just won. The warlock backed away from the waters in the pool of porphyry that was his window on the world. He turned and addressed his aeon-dead leman's pile of bones.

"Now Valhia! You can truly live again as my consort I knew in ages fell past! And I can again live as a man..."

Yet, Xexor-Wroth was unaware of the talisman lost where no moonlight gleamed.

## CHAPTER VII

## A WORLD GONE INSANE

Tawna paced about the clearing looking for Vegtam. The Skald was nowhere to be seen. She imagined the ground trembling beneath her feet again and shook her head. Was she losing her mind? But a short while ago, they had been attacked by a giant scorpion formed of ruby. Had the whole world gone insane since the coming of the snake-men to Herod-Thaar?

Tawna furrowed her brow and tried to make sense of her situation. She had been shaken to the earth and knocked unconscious, but for how long?

When she awoke, Vegtam was gone, but surely the thing had happened. Trees lay uprooted upon the ground. The horses were gone. Had they run off in the upheaval or had the monster eaten them?

Tawna felt dizzy and put the back of her hand to her head, and as she did, her bare foot stepped on something sharp. She winced and reached down to pick up the object. She held it up before her eyes. It was the crystal talisman. Vegtam must have lost it during the monster's attack. *If Vegtam yet lives, and surely he must, this might help him vanquish the evil that had befallen him.* She had to find Vegtam!

There came a crash from the thicket immediately behind her. Torches blazed through the fogbound trees, and there were sounds of horses' hooves and men talking. She hid herself behind a large pine and fastened the pouch containing the talisman to a thick corded necklace that hung about her neck, stashing it inside her top.

The horses stopped, and Tawna heard a man say, "Well, they couldn't have gone much further than this. And if that fool General Harthin hadn't turned tail and fled back to Herod-Thaar the minute the Valley of Nephasth was mentioned, the musician would be hanging by his thumbs over a fire right now and you men would be enjoying that tavern whore." Tawna recognized the man's voice: Count Amschauld!

"Well Harthin is no longer a man, let alone a general, after having his face melted by acid, his manhood chopped off, and his skin stripped away! And that is what any one of you who turns yellow on me now will get—and worse!"

All was silent for a moment before Tawna heard the Count say, "Hold that torch over here! According to my map, the ruins of Nephasth lie northwesterly. That direction!" he snapped impatiently.

The horses were moving again, and Tawna circled the tree trunk hoping to remain out of sight as the men rode by. She looked after them as they disappeared past the copse of trees up ahead and out of view.

## CHAPTER VIII

## THE SORCERER'S ORCHARD

*How much did I drink last night?* This was Vegtam's first thought as consciousness slowly returned. He felt like his veins were on fire. His nerve endings crackled with pain.

His eyelids were heavy as lead, but he slowly managed to open them. He sat in a propped-up position. His eyes adjusted to the dimness, and he could see an orchid mist surrounding him. He tried to move but was held fast. He looked down and saw thick, pliable tendrils of crystal binding him at his wrists and ankles.

There was some slack in the restraints. He tried to stand, but the tendrils pulled taut, and he fell back into a sitting position. Vegtam strained his limbs to snap his restraints, but to no avail. He heard deep, rumbling laughter vibrating at his back. He looked up at a quartz Irminsul holding him captive. The massive, translucent bole contained a milky-white mist that shifted and flowed inside the thing's trunk. A gaping mouth in the pillar emitted yet another hilarity, then shut itself in silence.

Vegtam seemed to be in an open orchard lying beneath a crimson sky. Two black orbs hung suspended high above, beaming down purple rays into the darkness. He couldn't discern whether they were suns or moons.

He looked around, taking in the sights of an uncanny botanical nightmare. Sounds of suffering issued forth from all directions. One man—bound to the ground in a supine position—screamed in agony as crimson and black velvet-like tulips burst through his skin and rapidly grew bronze-colored suction cups on the ends. The sentient flowers attached themselves to the man's wounds and drank greedily of the blood trickling from the holes they had made sprouting from the man's flesh.

Vegtam looked away. When he did, he saw a naked emerald woman with long silver tresses. The green woman was surrounded by thick, hairy orange plants extending myriad tentacles like an octopus. The woman screamed as the intruders violated her every orifice. She trembled and twitched in her death throes.

Vegtam gritted his teeth and looked away. All about him towered more of the Irminsuls formed of solid crystal. From the sentient pillars hung cocoons spun of long, quartz leaves lined with blood-red veins. The cocoons were wrapped in human-shapes, and some of them emitted muffled protests and restrained, shrill cries. The wicked faces in the Irminsuls twisted ecstatically with perverse pleasure, and some of them laughed. Crystal spores fell from the wriggling cocoons.

Naked human bodies grew out of the ground. One side of them was that of a rotting corpse, and the other a crystalline plant with receding human features. Some of them were more pellucid than human, but still retained the shape of a man or woman. A few of them had solidified wholly into human-shaped quartz figures.

Vegtam shut his eyes against the madness that surrounded him and covered his ears with the little motion his crystal shackles afforded him. A door he hadn't seen opened into the misty orchid Hel, where Vegtam reclined unwillingly under the strange carmine sky.

A figure cloaked and hooded in a red robe entered and stood before Vegtam. Large talons reached up and brushed back its hood. Vegtam could see veins through the thing's waxy, translucent skin. Short, parchment-colored horns like those of a young goat sprouted from the top of the figure's head, and his face was set in a rictus drunk from aeons of evil. Gaunt though he was, his movements were lithesome and exuded power. His eyes burned a livid yellow.

The creature spoke in a sepulchral rasp, "Greetings, unfortunate one. I am Xexor-Wroth. I seek the Key to the Rune Realms. You are of no importance to me once I have it, and you can die a swift and painless death, though die you will. I saw you in the waters of Vysperia wherein I prophesy. You helped the priest of Odin slay my Aklo, further detaining my possession of the talisman." The sorcerer paused and ran his tongue out and flicked it in an age-old gesture of devil-worship and mockery of all that is wholesome.

"The irony of life for a mortal man is that it seems to play itself out backwards. When one is young, he is too foolish to live; and when he is old and has gained wisdom, he hasn't the energy to implement it. Not that it matters in your case, but I will tell you that life is made up of time. Unfortunate for you, you helped the Odin priest and delayed me in obtaining the Key. You have wasted *my* time. Now you hide the Key from me. But I will have it! Your time is nigh, but I think you will find that it will seem overlong even at the end of your life if you do not tell me where you have hidden the talisman—immediately!"

Vegtam growled and started to rise, but the vine-like tendrils yanked hard on his limbs and brought him to his knees. He gritted his teeth and barked at the sorcerer, "I know not of this talisman of which you speak, devil, and before this is over you will feel the wrath of the Æsir blood."

"Seek not to cozen me, one whose life is but the length of a sigh compared to my own!" snapped Xexor-Wroth.

Another tendril lashed out and gripped Vegtam by the throat, making it impossible for him to speak. Xexor-Wroth stood back and kicked at the barren earth before Vegtam and spat there. He held out his long clawed talons and made cryptic signs over the disturbed soil. A crystal bole burst up from the ground and sprouted flexible limbs that wriggled and waved as if in jubilant mockery of the dead and dying in the sorcerer's orchard.

"You dare threaten me, Xexor-Wroth, with Æsir wrath?" the warlock shouted. "I will show you why I am named as such! Now, you can be like the Odin Priest!"

Xexor-Wroth raised his arm, and his sleeve rolled back as he stretched forth his black-nailed talon and pointed at Vegtam. A wriggling quartz limb whipped forward from the Irminsul and pierced Vegtam's right eye. Acidic smoke billowed from the crackling socket where Vegtam's ruined eye shriveled and sizzled to naught. The Irminsul released its grip on

Vegtam's throat so the sorcerer could hear him scream.

Xexor-Wroth laughed and said, "This is only the beginning. I go now to look again into the waters of Vysperia for the talisman, and if I don't find it, you will lose another organ or limb each time I have to open the door to this chamber!"

With a wave of the warlock's hand, the adamantine quartz bonds jerked Vegtam aloft. From behind the translucent bole, the wicked Irminsul brought around more of its crystal tendrils like whips and lashed Vegtam to the translucent tree where he hung. Vegtam clenched his teeth in agony, and so great was the pain of losing his eye that consciousness receded and he fell back into utter darkness. The Irminsul roared with mocking laughter, and Xexor-Wroth joined in with his own cachinnations.

## CHAPTER IX

## IN THE RUINS OF NEPHASTH

Spiraled towers leaned drunkenly in the light of the full moon which shone on jeweled minarets. Impractical angles suggested an alien architecture engineered by a hand skilled in bizarre, hellish geometry. The riders shivered when they looked upon the ruins of Nephasth. Most of them had heard the tales of the wars of wizardry fought with chemicals and magick in ages long gone, and they wondered at what immortal abominations given birth by such gramarye might still lurk in creeping shadows.

"They have to be hiding somewhere in this vicinity." Count Amschauld swept his arm, indicating the ruined temples and collapsing structures about the avenue. "They would have made camp at nightfall, and we spotted no horses along the way, so that minstrel and the whore have to be here. I want every building searched and not a stone left unturned until we find them.

"Tarrak, give the horses more *kreesap*. You know they didn't like being around the snake-men back at the pass. And double the dose for my horse. He has always been a nervous fellow," Amschauld said.

Amschauld dismounted and turned to a soldier clad in casque and byrnie. "Galdruth, take half the men and start there." He pointed across the road to downfallen blocks and scattered shards that could have once been a mansion. "Ortun, you and the rest of the men, come with me. No telling what we might run into, but I have a few tricks of my own and one really big one.

"General Ophiolater has the pass entering Nephasth guarded with his snake-men. If by some chance of fortune those two try to ride back in the

## THE SNAKE-MAN'S BANE

direction of Herod-Thaar, the snake-men will intercept them there."

Amschauld shifted his torch to his left hand, and his right hand wrenched sword from scabbard. He paused in front of the moss-covered edifice supported by enormous columns on either side. With a nod of his head, he gestured for the men to follow him through the portico.

---

Xexor-Wroth stepped back from the waters of Vysperia where he had just seen Count Amschauld and his men enter the city. The sorcerer growled like a wild animal. For the moment, he forgot the Key to the Rune Realms.

Had the warlock stared a moment longer into the water boiling inside the igneous formation, he would have seen a lone figure trailing Amschauld's men on a great black stallion. For as luck would have it for Tawna, she had come across Vegtam's steed when she set out on foot with torch in hand in the direction Amschauld had indicated for his men to follow.

"Who dares invade the demesne of Xexor-Wroth? No one has done so for ages! And now these fools shall learn why!"

Xexor-Wroth held his hands up to either side of his face with the palms inward and straight. He stepped into a stance emulating a god-form—an ancient thing dwelling in the outer gulfs of time and space and long forgotten by men, but not forgotten by Xexor-Wroth.

The shape of the warlock's transparent face shifted. His old bones cracked, and his body rearranged its shape. As it did so, he ran. Faster and faster he fled down corridors, and his robe fell from him in tatters even as his bones reset themselves. Soon, the sorcerer was no more a man but a giant hairless rat, racing forth with transparent flesh through which the blood visibly pumped like fluids in a crisscrossing, complex series of alchemist's tubes.

---

Tawna tethered her mount to a dust-choked fountain that stood in what surely had once been a bazaar in another age. She weaved her way on foot through broken architraves and pillars, ducking in and out of the debris to avoid detection. She arrived just in time to see Count Amschauld and his men split up. Amschauld entered the only edifice in the square with its roof intact. If there was life amongst the ruins of Nephasth, it was likely to be there.

Tawna crept furtively along, keeping a safe distance between herself and the blazing torches of the men in front of her. She could hear them speaking but not what they were saying. Ahead of her the men came to a wall with corridors leading off to left and right. Amschauld and his men went right. Tawna resolved to follow them and extinguished her torch.

Tawna paced herself and gave the men time to move ahead, hoping to remain unseen. Suddenly, she heard a scratching like enormous claws racing through the corridor off to her left. As she threw herself back against the wall of the adjoining corridor, she caught a quick glimpse of a monstrous shape running by. The thing looked like a giant translucent rat made of wax.

There was a crash up ahead, and men screamed. Steel hissed free of scabbards, and she could hear men dying wholesale as they brandished their weapons. Tawna ran to where the corridors intersected and looked down the hall. She could see what lay before her in the light of myriad torches. Up ahead, men were slaughtered like cattle. The giant hairless rat bowed its back, haunches raised high above and paws on the floor like a dog in a playful stance. A man's head was in the monster's mouth. It showed two rows of saw-like teeth and clamped down on the head. A sound issued forth like the cracking of a large nut, and blood jetted out of the man's thorax as the colossal rat came away with its morsel. Men crowded about the creature, attacking with sword and spear, but to no avail. The weapons seldom found their mark, and when they did, the rat's pierced flesh healed over sooner than they could strike anew.

The giant rat darted about the soldiers with uncanny speed, rending and tearing limbs from the dying men. Two soldiers thrust spears at the creature as a third man ran and dove onto its back, raising his sword high above his head and stabbing between the rat's shoulder blades. The creature reared and screeched so loudly that some of the men dropped their weapons and covered their ears. The soldier on the rat's back squatted, putting all his weight onto his sword and shoved it deeper into the creature. The rat flipped over on its back, and bones crunched. The rat rolled upright, chittering as with laughter, and revealed the dead warrior it had just crushed. It swatted at the man's lifeless form, drawing his corpse closer to it. With its other claw, it ripped the dead man's torso open and held the man up like an obscene doll to show the others how they were made.

Tawna flattened herself against the wall and held her breath as the remainder of Amschauld's troops rounded the adjoining corridor and raced down the hall toward the din of battle. From the ruined edifice nearby, the others had heard the tumult and joined the remainder of the men engaged in combat with the monster. The soldiers paused for only a moment, and the thing was again amongst them, slashing throats with its saw-like teeth, ripping and rending limbs and tearing still-beating hearts from chests.

Amschauld shouted commands that fell on deaf ears in the pandemonium. The Count seethed with rage, and his beady eyes glared at the colossus before him. This was no mere atavist that had survived the ages when colossi stalked the earth. This was a thing born of sorcery and possessing a keen intelligence.

Amschauld stood with his feet close together at the back of the last line of his soldiers and folded his arms. Closing his eyes and relaxing amidst the carnage, his lips moved as though he were singing a song. His body shuddered as with an ague for a moment, and then his movements became wavering and serpentine. His face stretched and contorted—elongated. His helmet toppled from his head. Black pupils rolled over and filled the opened eye slits. Jupon and armor fell away, and his body spun out coils as Amschauld left his armor and weapons in a pile on the floor.

He slithered forth towards the giant rat, and the soldiers parted way. Some of them had heard of the transformation, but most of them had never seen Amschauld's shape-shifting in action. They stood by as Amschauld, now an enormous serpent, glided across the floor. His forked tongue flickered. His shiny green skin and gold and black mottling gleamed in the faint torchlight. The men cleared a path between the monsters. The snake undulated and coiled, ready to strike. The giant rat stepped back as if ready to spring but instead skittered up the wall into a high alcove looking down upon the corridor.

With a screech, the giant, hairless rodent opened its mouth. Blood pumped through the veins and arteries of its body and came out its mouth, and it spat down onto the soldiers standing closest to it, spears at the ready. The men screamed as the rat's plasma burned away their flesh like acid raining down on them.

The giant serpent hissed and dislocated its jaw. A loud cracking of bones came from the alcove above as the rat's features shifted. Its body grew longer, and the proportions ballooned. It sprouted thick iron-grey fur all over, and its tail became the same length as its body. It breathed hard as Xexor-Wroth called on all of his reserves to quickly generate anti-venom receptors.

The creature was the largest mongoose Tawna had ever seen. The massive snake struck at the mongoose, but the mongoose was quicker and was already behind the serpent, grabbing the snake by the tail and flinging it around. The snake hit the wall with a blow that shook the entire corridor.

Tawna had seen enough. She ran in the opposite direction while soldiers were preoccupied with the battling colossi. Right now, anywhere was better than where she was. She could feel the blows resonating from far down the corridor as the floor trembled beneath her. The ceiling cracked, and white powder fell down on her. She ran and ran but could still hear the hiss of the enormous snake and the screech of the giant mongoose in the distance. She could hear men screaming as they were crushed by the two warring abominations. The battle ebbed and flowed. It followed her at a distance, but follow her it did.

## CHAPTER X

## THE GUARDIAN OF THE RUNE REALMS

*I know myself hanging on the wind-cold tree for nine icy nights,*
*Wounded by the spear consecrated to Wodan, I consecrated to myself.*
*I was hanging on the mighty tree, which conceals man, where man grew out of its roots.*
*They offered me neither bread nor wine, so I bent down in search.*
*I recognized the Runes, and shrieking, I grasped them until I sank down from the tree.*
*Now, I began to increase and to be wise, to grow and to feel well.*
*From the word, word grew after word, and work shaped on work to works.*
*Now, I know the songs like no wise woman and none of the children of man.*
*And should those songs, o human child, be unlearnable to you for sheer endless time,*
*Grasp them, once you get hold of them—*
*Bless you if you retain them!*
*- Odin's Rune Song*

Tawna rounded a corner into a much larger space. Lamps suspended on brackets were fastened to the wall and cast light about the hall. Therein were doors to four antechambers.

Tawna's ample bosom rose and fell quickly as she sucked in air. Irresolute, she looked about. She didn't know which way to go. She felt a warm tingling between her breasts and put her hand down her top, retrieving the talisman the Odin Priest had given to Vegtam. She looked down at the object, and one of the runes glowed. She held the crystal tightly in her right fist and heard words spoken in her head by a voice that was not her own. *Go left!* the foreign voice said.

Strange caryatids shattered on the floor and pillars cracked in the hallway as the battle between the two monsters grew closer. Tawna obeyed the voice. She spied the room to her left, and she parted tapestries upon which were depicted scenes of women and chimeras in obscene acts. Quickly she entered a chamber. The room was faintly illuminated by an orchid radiance in the wall outlining a door. Tawna again heard the strange voice in her head. *Open the door.*

Tawna felt for a handle, but there was none. *Just push it*, the foreign voice said.

Tawna pressed the door and felt it give way. As soon as she opened the door, she could hear the howling of the damned. Inside the room she looked upon another world. She was afraid, but the voice told her, *Go ahead. He is waiting.*

Tawna put her right foot forward and stepped down into a hellish orchard. The otherworldly plane was illuminated by two black orbs in the sky casting down a brilliant purple effulgence. Inside the orchid-lit orchard stood great crystal boles upon which hung quartz cocoons wherein human-shaped things struggled and cried out in agony. The door slammed behind Tawna, and she cried out and felt frantically for the wall, but it was gone. There was no sign that an opening to the world had ever existed.

*Don't mind that. Go to him! Quickly!* said the voice in Tawna's head. She looked around to see what the voice referred to, and she spied a man hanging on a tree off to her left.

"Vegtam!" she cried. The man's head rolled over in her direction. He had only one eye. Tawna broke into a run towards Vegtam, but a crystalline vine lashed out from a nearby tree and entwined the woman's ankle. A mouth opened in the Irminsul and emitted wicked laughter. More of the bole's quartz tendrils lashed about her limbs and torso, dragging her towards the thing's open mouth. Tawna looked fearfully upon the jagged crystals showing in the thing's food hole and winced. More of the Irminsuls nearby joined her attacker in a cacophony of hilarities. Grunting and straining, she braced herself against its trunk with arms and legs. She was being fed alive to the crystalline abhorrence.

Calmly, the voice came again in her head. *Touch it with the talisman.* As soon as the object touched the Irminsul, it closed its mouth and shrank back in fear. The thing's tendrils released Tawna, and with a thump she fell to the ground and rolled over to where Vegtam hung. She still gripped the talisman tightly in her hand.

Tawna stood and held up her hand to touch Vegtam, but he didn't respond. Dried blood filled the socket where his eye had once set and his clothes were in tatters. *Has he perished hanging in this abominable orchard of monstrosities?* Weeping, she unclenched her fist and the talisman vibrated. It was warm, and runes glowed in its crystalline depths, reaching into other worlds. Vegtam's head rolled, and he moaned, tried to speak. More of the runes on the talisman glowed, and the quartz tendrils that bound Vegtam to the devilish Irminsul relinquished their hold on him. With a scream he fell to the ground, then raised himself to his knees.

"The talisman," he mumbled through parched lips. "Give me the Key."

Tawna held her hand out to Vegtam, and he took the Key to the Rune Realms and shoved it into the empty socket that had once housed his eye. At first he cried out; then a sense of warmth passed through him like heady liquor coursing through his veins. Pain, hunger, thirst, fear: all vanished from him, and yet the sensation of strong liquor swimming in his veins came again, but this time tenfold.

He pushed himself up on wobbly legs and strained to speak. "A third song I know, which is good to me… for a fetter to my enemies. I dull the steel of my foes… so that their swords…will cut no more."

He felt a rush of power go up his spine like a crack of lightning. The talisman told him what to do. He staggered upright and brought the tips of his thumb and ring finger of his left hand together. The rest of his fingers pointed upward. "Th-Th-Thorn…" he chanted.

That was all he could get out. It was as if the Guardian of the Rune Realms had been waiting to take over. Tawna drew back in fear as Vegtam sank to his knees, screaming and growling like a maddened beast. The talisman glowed inside of Vegtam's eye socket. He looked upon dim vistas far beyond the ken of man. He saw before him runic characters forming worlds within worlds. He saw the wyverns, the giant white spiders with demon heads, and the horrible grotesqueries that swam about and screamed in a pre-human land of fire, darkness, and primordial soup when man was still but a dream. Anon, man arose from primal slime and walked forward, still in his infancy of beasthood. The runes flashed forth through the nine angles, and Vegtam saw the nine worlds cut from the Rune Realms of creation and come into being.

Vegtam's spine readjusted itself, and he grew in stature and girth. His skin turned the color of snow, and his skull and cheekbones cracked and reset themselves. Two horns burst from his head, dipping down and thrusting back up in defiance of the two black orbs that loomed high above this world wherein he had been immured. The sable discs cast their purple rays down on the hateful grimace that spread over his countenance. Long hair the color of blood spilled over his massive shoulders. Sinews of steel rippled when he drew forth his mighty broadsword. He stood nearly seven feet tall. With both clawed hands, he raised the massive glaive high, throwing his head back and laughing maniacally.

Tawna shuddered and shrank back. "Vegtam?" she asked the demon.

"I am Thorn, the Rune incarnate. I guard the Rune Realms. I am borrowing Vegtam for a time. We now hold discourse. There is important work to be done. Fear not, woman! Vegtam will be returned to you unharmed, for he is of the Æsir blood. Let us leave this place!"

With that, Thorn gripped his broadsword two-handed and hacked at the open air in the hellish orchard. There he cleft a jagged hole connecting the world of Xexor-Wroth's orchard with that of the wizard's mansion in the ruins of Nephasth. Thorn stepped through the newly-carved door connecting the worlds and led Tawna into the antechamber where she had first entered that secret place. A wind blew fiercely against them, blowing back Thorn's crimson mane and Tawna's raven locks. Thorn turned and brushed his hand over the door he had cut, restoring the antechamber. The wind ceased to howl, and there was no sign of that other world.

Thorn cocked his head and listened, as if the Rune could hear before the sound was made; there was a loud thumping in the hallway. Thorn stepped out of the antechamber into the great hall. Before him a colossal serpent writhed in its death throes. The snake had gashes all along its oily green skin. Chunks were missing from its scales, showing ruined patterns of gold and black mottling where green ichor seeped in puddles throughout the hall. The dying abomination flopped about, hitting the walls as dust fell from the ceiling. Thorn's red eyes were like two burning rubies penetrating the murky darkness beyond the dying snake's body. There sat a giant mongoose returning his gaze with its fiery amber stare.

Thorn sheathed his sword and growled in rage. Tawna stepped aside as Thorn hefted the colossal serpent and tossed it behind him. Its skull slammed against the wall, cracking loudly as it crushed that section of the building. The snake lay still—expired.

When Thorn turned again to face the mongoose, it was gone; and in its place stood a man, if he could be called that. He was naked, and his flesh was nearly rotted away by aeons of demonic invocation. Thorn could see the heart beating, pumping blood through the veins and arteries of the creature. He could see the lungs working quickly and the rotten organs in the thing's body. The Rune chuckled, and it sounded like the gruff bark of a big dog. Thorn cocked his head sideways and looked at Xexor-Wroth.

"So, wizard, you think to invade the Rune Realms." It was a statement, not a question.

"I have summoned many demons," Xexor-Wroth stated. "And I have had many summoned against me. Yet, here I still stand. I know you are from the Rune Realms. Likely you attached yourself to the pure creative energies and sallied forth when the portal leading back here was opened."

The silence was oppressively thick. Thorn stood still as a statue.

Xexor-Wroth's voice grated like the rusty hinges on an age-old sarcophagus. "I have banished many demons in my time. Though your origin is unknown to me, you will go screaming back to Hel as all of the others who have served me have done." With this, Xexor-Wroth raised his arms as quickly as a panther, and a burst of levin shot forth and crackled from his talons. Thorn raised one hand, and the lightning bolt died in midair.

Xexor-Wroth's eyes blazed livid yellow fire. He chanted, "Lilitu, Lamiae, Xycanthia! Naamah, Adriel, Ansitif! Open Nuctemeron, cross Choronzon, come forth!"

A lavender mist formed between Xexor-Wroth and Thorn. Out of the mist walked a silver-skinned woman with deep cobalt hair and almond-shaped eyes full of jet. She stood before Thorn and fixed him with a wanton gaze. Thorn crossed his arms and showed no sign of interest. She then let fall her silken, saffron robe revealing round melon-like breasts and shapely thighs. She smiled, and fangs came to points inside her red lips. Thorn lashed out and backhanded the succubus, and she lay writhing on the floor. He then took her by her dark blue tresses and hacked at her neck with his sword. With one blow the demon's head came free, and Thorn tossed it away insouciantly.

It was then that Thorn noticed the black wheels spinning along the length of the sorcerer's person. These masses of energy twirled in the forehead, the throat, the heart area, the stomach, and the groin region on the wizard's decaying body. There was a loud humming, and tendrils exploded forth and branched out, taking Thorn by the throat. Thorn grimaced momentarily and the wizard began drawing energy out of Thorn back into himself.

"If I can't send you back to the pit, I can certainly feed on your energy and drain you dry, demon!" said Xexor-Wroth.

Thorn laughed as a man who thoroughly appreciates his own jest—even if no one else in the room does—and Xexor-Wroth knew in that instant that the demon's cachinnations carried with them an ill portent, for the energy began flowing from Xexor-Wroth like spilled wine into Thorn's massive frame. Too late, Xexor-Wroth realized that Thorn was far too powerful for the warlock's magicks. Tawna watched, eyes wide in wondrous horror as Thorn drank the very essence of the sorcerer and pulled Xexor-Wroth's dying body to him by the ethereal tendrils that the wizard had attacked Thorn with.

Appalled and fascinated at the same time, Tawna came closer to get a better look. The amber lights that had once glowed in Xexor-Wroth's eyeholes flickered as if candles in the wind. His head rolled to the side, and he glimpsed Tawna.

"Valhia," Xexor-Wroth mumbled. "My Valhia." He reached out his hand, then his form went limp.

Thorn gripped the sorcerer's head in his mighty clutches and wrenched head from body. It made an awful sound like the rending of coarse fabric.

Not a drop of blood escaped the wizard's corpse. Thorn tore off Xexor-Wroth's arms and legs and laughed as he destroyed the sorcerer like a mean boy with a ragdoll. When he was finished, he threw the pieces of Xexor-Wroth on the floor with a grunt of satisfaction.

"What did he mean when he called me 'Valhia?'" Tawna asked Thorn.

"You are likely someone he knew in one of your past incarnations."

Tawna opened her mouth as if to ask another question, but Thorn interrupted her. "It is better not to know more. These things are often painful and confusing." Thorn kicked the dead wizard's remains into a pile on the floor and turned to go.

Tawna looked after him in abject horror. "Where is Vegtam?"

"He is in here with me. He tells me things," the Rune replied.

"Bring him back!" Tawna commanded.

"In good time," Thorn snorted. "Right now Vegtam and I have some business to attend to." Thorn turned and began walking away.

"Where are you going?" Tawna shouted.

"To the city—Herrod-Thaar."

"But Herod-Thaar is crawling with snake-men. An army of them guard the pass leading from Nephasth back to the city. I heard Count Amschauld himself say as much."

"Aye, woman. That is why I am bound for the pass."

"To do battle with a whole army?" she exclaimed.

"Aye. To do battle with the whole army."

"But why?"

"Because they are my hereditary enemies. I have fought them before the world you know was even the dream of an insane god. Their wyrd is upon them now."

"What of the soldiers that remain in the ruins of Nephasth?" Tawna asked.

Thorn sniffed the dank air. "All dead."

"All dead?"

"All dead but us." Thorn's face split into a hateful grin.

Tawna shivered. "The battle between the giant snake and the giant mongoose. The rest must have perished in the pandemonium."

Without another word, Thorn turned and strode through the corridors of the dead sorcerer's mansion, and Tawna ran to keep up with him.

## CHAPTER XI

## THE SNAKE-MAN'S BANE

The late afternoon sun glinted on burnished helmets, silver breastplates, gilt-worked mail, and gleaming weapons along the horizon. Thorn cast his burning red gaze upon the sinuous shapes that mocked mankind in his own accoutrements of war: the serpent who walked upright like a man—the snake-man. Thorn rode closer and turned Vegtam's night-black stallion to make sure they could get a good look at Tawna sitting on the back of the mount.

"Your paramour does not fancy you being used for bait," Thorn growled. The Rune could feel Tawna trembling at the prospect of being taken by the army of snake- men lining the ridge in the distance.

Thorn drew his mighty broadsword and pointed it at the snake-men. The Rune whipped his sword overhead, and the great black steed reared and beat the air with its hooves. He saw a figure step forth and stare into the valley below where Thorn issued his challenge. Thorn snorted, surmising this was their leader. The snake-man shouted to his troops and gestured wildly with his arms, hissing commands.

"What now?" Tawna said, her voice trembling.

"We wait. It won't take them as long as it would a man to traverse the gorge. Vegtam told me of the narrow defile debouching onto the floor of the valley. There I shall wait. At the end of the path will be the snake-man's bane!"

---

The sun was setting when Thorn dismounted. "Ride back toward the wizard's manse. Do you remember the cave I indicated on the way here?"

"Yes," Tawna replied.

"Hide yourself away there. Do not return to the pass until dusk."

"But what if the battle does not go as you plan? Might you not need the steed to flee?"

"I have never left a battle until all my enemies lay dead."

Tawna started to protest but Thorn interposed, "Hie to the cave. Do not return to the pass until dusk."

Tawna raked the horse's ribs with the heels of her boots, and the stallion reared and whinnied. She held tightly to the reins and managed to get the beast under control. The horse ran a few yards, and Tawna brought it to a stop and turned to look at Thorn where he stood watching the pass in the waning sunlight, his blood-red hair whipping in the wind. The sun seemed not to touch where steel sinews bulged beneath alabaster skin. He looked like a Nordic demon chiseled from fine marble by a bloodthirsty master sculptor.

Tawna paused for a moment, then turned Vegtam's steed and raced off in the direction of the cave.

---

The first snake-man to reach the floor of the valley hissed a bloodcurdling scream as Thorn cleft his skull in twain with his broadsword. The pass was so narrow that only one snake-man could exit the gorge at a time. Though they did so hastily, Thorn's sword licked out like levin and drove through the torso of the next reptilian to step over the body of his fallen comrade. A third snake-man approached, wicked curved scimitar glistening in the light of the setting sun. Before the reptilian could swing his steel, Thorn hacked serpentine head from sinuous body. Green ichor spurted from the thing's neck.

Thorn slashed and stabbed and heaped the carnage high. The mouth of the pass filled with reptilian corpses and the stench of dead serpent flesh. Thorn had long ago silenced the voice of Vegtam, whom he now possessed and replaced with his own physical manifestation on Earth. He didn't need the distraction of the Skald's concerns regarding his goal of extinction for the snake-man.

Thorn's consciousness extended outward like ripples in a large body of water traversing a great distance. Because of this, he could hear thoughts and speech from afar. Anon, he heard a sibilant hissing, "You there! Scale the wall and drop down on him!" It was the leader of the snake-men issuing commands back up the gorge. Thorn saw a dark horde of sinuous shapes in his mind's eye, so the attack held no surprise for the Rune when two snake-men dropped down behind him as he thrust his sword through the enemy in front of him. He immediately withdrew his blade and hacked his next foe to the breast bone. With a backhanded arc, Thorn lashed out and slashed to his rear. His attacker's head spun through the air like a top. Before it could hit the ground, the Rune dealt another death blow to the second would-be assassin coming up from behind.

Thorn turned his attention back to the pass. The snake-men lay dead in heaps. Their fellows climbed over them in their reptilian fashion, half-walking, half-slithering. Two snake-men were now approaching since the Rune had been forced to defend his back. Thorn split the skull of the first one to reach him and leaned back as the second snake-man grazed the Rune's snow-white flesh across his shoulder with his scimitar. Thorn responded with a thrust that disemboweled the reptilian, and the snake-man's innards spilled upon the ground. Green ichor lay in pools all about the pass, where the snake-men bled out in their death throes. Thorn only bled from minor cuts here and there where the snake-men's blades had managed to find purchase, for what it was worth. By his own vital force, the Rune's body healed his wounds as he fought on.

The sun had set when Tawna rode upon the slaughter. The narrow mouth debouching upon the verdant sward was heaped high with snake-men corpses. A few had made it over the high wall and had been delivered unto the eternal shadows by Thorn's broadsword—the same as their fellows attacking from the mouth of the pass.

Thorn mowed down two snake-men like chaff before the scythe when two more reptilians managed to drop from the high wall and land behind him. Tawna cried out, "Thorn behind you!" but the Rune was already facing his foes. He delivered a blow that split the first snake-man from shoulder to breast and hacked the second snake-man's blade in twain with the return, knocking the reptilian to the ground.

Before he could slay the snake-man on the ground, he heard Tawna cry out. The two reptilians to the rear had her. It was at this moment that Vegtam managed to break through the surface from somewhere deep within where Thorn had hidden him. The Skald screamed, "Tawna! No!"

Three more snake-men had managed to break through the wall of dead reptilian bodies barricading the mouth of the gorge. Thorn easily pushed Vegtam back down, and the Skald submerged within the depths of the Rune's vast and alien consciousness. It was just long enough for the three snake-men to simultaneously leap onto the Rune and drive their daggers into him. Two more dropped from the high wall of rock and joined them. As they pulled Thorn to the ground, he heard a voice within his broad sense of perception from back up the gorge. Their general hissed a desperate cry, "Fall back! The way is blocked by the dead. We face a demon this day! Not a man, but a demon! Fall back! Make for Herod-Thaar to live and fight another day!" Unbeknownst to the general, a handful of his soldiers had managed to drag the Rune down onto the sward, but the rest of the snake-men were already retreating back up the gorge.

The two snake-men holding fast to Tawna taunted her. "She will make a fine breeder for Granlamb's seraglio." His fellow chortled and hissed, "Just look at those wide birthing hips and large breasts," he said, flicking his forked tongue. "I wager you she can give enough milk to feed several baby emperors at a time."

Tawna growled like a wildcat and spat in the reptilian's eye. He drew his hand back but his comrade excitedly hissed, "Not the touch of venom, Granlamb will want her…" but he never finished speaking.

## THE SNAKE-MAN'S BANE

A bestial roar filled the valley, accompanied by the sickening crunch and bursting of entrails and the sound of wrenching limbs. The bodies of dead and dying snake-men flew in all directions as Thorn stood, holding his steel with both hands and whipping the slimy green snake-men's blood from the blade. Blood seeped from myriad wounds upon his massive torso, but he cared not. Already his wounds healed. One might easier kill a demon of Hades than to drag down unto death the Guardian of the Rune Realms whom was himself the Thorn Rune incarnate.

The two snake-men flung Tawna upon the ground and raced towards Thorn. Tawna raised herself up, and with wide eyes she watched the butchery before her, for it certainly was not a fight. With successive strokes that looked like they came from a world where time moved differently—much faster—Thorn severed both arms from the first snake-man to meet him. He laughed mirthlessly as the reptilian fell to its knees. The green ichor that was the thing's blood spurted. Thorn's blade whistled through the air, and the snake-man's head went flying from his shoulders. The second snake-man arrived just in time to have his blade hacked in twain. With another blow from Thorn's sword that was a blur to the snake-man, the Rune slashed both legs from underneath the reptilian. The creature tumbled like a falling tower and lay on its belly, writhing.

Thorn addressed the now legless snake-man mockingly, "And so shall you go on your belly and eat dust all the days of your life." Thorn's face split into a hateful rictus, and with fists gripping the hilt of his broadsword he drove the point of his blade down into the reptilian's skull. The Rune twisted his blade with both hands, and the reptilian's skull shattered. Green, slimy blood and brains splattered out upon the ichor-soaked sward.

Thorn sheathed his sword and made a series of gestures in the air conjuring a bind-rune. Anon, there came a rumble of wheels, and presently a golden chariot appeared, drawn by enormous black goats with spiral horns and glowing red eyes. The chariot was ornate and inscribed with runes, but by its sturdy build it was obviously a war machine.

Tawna gasped in awe at the thing. Without a word, Thorn swept Tawna off her feet and leapt into the chariot with the woman under one arm. He roared a command, and the goats turned the car around and ran some paces before Thorn bellowed another command. At Thorn's guttural utterance, the goats made a sharp angle and pulled the chariot toward the mountain.

Wide eyed with fright, Tawna cried out, "Where are you taking me?"

"Up the mountainside, woman!" Thorn gripped her tightly in the crook of his arm, his mighty thews like steel. With his other arm he held tirelessly to the crossbar as the car drew them up to dizzying heights.

"Why?" she screamed over the ruckus of the rumbling chariot wheels.

"To finish what I started! Not a snake-man is to be left alive in Herod-

Thaar! Vegtam told me you have a friend in the city. A tavern owner. You will go there."

"But what of Vegtam? Bring him back to me!"

"In good time. I told you Vegtam sleeps deep within; there he heals. I will leave you and him with the tavern owner while I do business in Herod-Thaar. I no longer require him as my vessel, but presently there is no time for his return. We must make haste, for tonight I have much death to deal.

"The slaughter of my age-old enemy in the Valley of Nephasth served a dual purpose. It was also a ritual to sustain my presence on this plane without the need of a host. This shall allow me to range here long enough to rid this demesne of the menace that walks upright on two legs when it should crawl on its belly and have its head crushed by a rock."

Tawna looked back over her shoulder at the receding valley below as they climbed higher and higher. She put her hand to her head, and swooning, fainted in the iron-grip of Thorn's arm. The chariot crawled quickly up the side of the mountain like a giant, deadly spider stalking its prey. And darkness fell and spread over the land.

## CHAPTER XII

## SON OF ODIN

Vegtam the Skald stood before that Vegtam of old — he who had ridden in with the Wild Hunt to young Vegtam's mother's abode in the days of the Skald's youth. Only now, the old Vegtam was clad in richly-worked golden armor engraved with runes and bind-runes. His white hair and beard fell over shoulders and chest, and his one blue eye burned majestically beneath his brow and fell upon the younger Vegtam.

The Skald addressed the old man. "You are that Vegtam who visited us long ago in my youth, are you not, sire? A wizard who kept company with my mother—the witch—upon occasion?"

The old man barked out a short laugh. "Aye, I am. But call me not a wizard, but the Father of Wizards, and call me the Father of the Gods, as well. I have been known by many names, Vegtam being the one I took when I wandered amongst men and got children upon the daughters of men. Your mother was such a one. I am Odin, and you are my son, and as such, you are of the Æsir blood."

Vegtam held his hand up to where his eye had once been. Inside the eyeless socket now set the Key to the Rune Realms. He looked puzzled.

"No, it is not a dream," Odin said. "It is real. You have sacrificed your eye, and you now possess knowledge like no wise woman and none of the children of man. You have encountered much that is strange in the world of men, and don't think this is the last of it. There will be many more adventures in your life before I call you to sit with your brothers in Valhalla."

"But I am a Skald, not a warrior."

"Nay, son. Your path is that of a Priest of Odin." He reached out a powerful hand and firmly gripped Vegtam's shoulder. "Your wyrd is the runes, and the runes are your songs. Blood flows where it needs to be shed. Guard well the Key to the Rune Realms. When you are in trouble, always look to the runes. They hold the answers. You must return to the world of men now. There are those who need you there.

"All of the snake-men are dead and the Emperor with them. Thorn led the Wild Hunt last night, and those lands that begat such malevolence have been cleansed by fire and steel. Visit again the lands of the North, where reside your people. Though, you will not stay long, for the wanderlust is upon you. Now go!"

With that Vegtam's one eye opened. Tawna laid her head upon his chest and wept with joy.

"Vegtam! Thank the gods! You are back. Just as Thorn said. I began to doubt the Rune's words, but he knew. He knew!"

Vegtam pulled Tawna to him and kissed her long and fiercely. After much display of affection between the two lovers, Tawna told Vegtam of the wild ride in Thorn's chariot and how the Rune had stepped out of Vegtam's inert form, leaving him collapsed upon the floor of Sargas Tuun's back room. She told him of how they had hidden themselves away in the subterranean chamber beneath The Proud Fool's Inn while death stalked the streets and palaces of Herod-Thaar; and how Thorn—the Rune incarnate—wreaked havoc upon the world of the snake-men and the children of Hewahay.

Vegtam told Tawna of his meeting with Odin and his father's words of prophecy. Tawna agreed that Vegtam should return to his homeland in the North and insisted that she accompany him. They made plans for traveling. They agreed they would invite Sargas Tuun to travel with them, if the innkeeper would go. He had been good to them, and Tawna feared for his safety if he remained in Herod-Thaar.

As Vegtam's earthly senses returned, it dawned on him that he and Tawna were in a room on the second floor of The Proud Fool's Inn.

After Tawna had given Vegtam the eyepatch Sargas Tuun had procured for him, the Skald dressed himself in silken garments of crimson and sable. His belly snarled like a tiger, and he growled, "I am hungry, and worse, I have been without strong drink for days!"

"Then, let's go downstairs and see what Sargas Tuun has to eat and drink," Tawna said.

Anon, Vegtam and Tawna made their way down the staircase of the tavern. Silence fell over the sparsely populated room at the sound of feet on the stairs. When the occupants saw that the creaking of the stairs had been caused by Tawna and the Skald, they went back to their business of drinking and gossiping, albeit in muffled tones. That is, save for two old men Vegtam instantly recognized from when he had first set foot in Sargas Tuun's establishment.

Vegtam's eye caught Tawna's, and he gestured to her with a nod of his head. They went to the table closest to Hunthar and Leric and sat down. Vegtam focused his keen, Skaldic sense of hearing on the conversation taking place between the two old men.

"Aye! Found Granlamb's head lying on the floor of his sleeping chamber. His body was still in the bed. Don't reckon he'll be getting up again," Hunthar said.

Leric chuckled, "The people of Herod-Thaar don't know whether to barricade themselves inside their homes or have a parade. They say it was a demon come roaring through the streets in a chariot last night. Said the car was pulled by two hellish goats with eyes that glowed like fire. Said 'fore long he was joined by a whole horde of demons, and war broke out on the snake-men. Now, it sounds to me like some of the folks of Herod-Thaar have been taking the opium pipe to bed with them, but something's damned sure afoot here. They ain't a snake-man been seen since last night. No soldiers roaming the streets, and those damned Mosuuls seem to be making themselves scarce, as well."

Hunthar nodded his head in agreement. "I reckon I'll be making for Thorkistani soon. No telling what might break out here, but civil war or worse is likely. Who knows? Draco Kharn might take a notion to come rolling over Herod-Thaar with his war chariots once he hears tell of Granlamb's untimely end."

"There is still the matter of a well-guarded border to cross. Same problem as before, Hunthar. Looks like you're stuck here. At least for a while."

"Not so. The border is clear," Vegtam spoke in a deep baritone. "And as it happens, Tawna and I are headed that way soon enough. You are welcome to come along if you like."

"How do you know this, Skald?" Leric shot back, making a sour face.

"I have wandered much, and I hear much. Sometimes I hear things from afar. In fact, so far as to you would scarce believe it. But I have it from a reliable source."

"Here is a man of the North, like my forefathers. By troth, I have no doubt he speaks truth." Hunthar smiled and raised his drinking jack to

Vegtam. "Buy you a drink, Northman?"

The corners of Vegtam's mouth formed a wry grin, and he nodded his head.

Tawna said, "Be careful what you promise, old man. If you start buying drinks for Vegtam, you may not have enough coin left to leave Herod-Thaar."

Hunthar stood and held aloft his cup. "To my new friend, Vegtam, and the Northern blood. And a round for everyone in the house—on me!"

The room came alive, and Leric raised his voice above the cacophony. "It's a good thing half of the town is still afraid to come out, or you would be begging alms in the street to pay for your drinking tab tonight, you drunk bastard."

The room erupted with laughter.

Hunthar called out to where everyone could hear him, shifting attention away from Leric's jest. "Hey Skald, how about a song?"

"I don't have a lute anymore. I broke it in a fight with Count Amschauld and a snake-man." Vegtam grinned, lolling comfortably in his chair.

An ominous silence swept the room. All that could be heard was the creaking of tables and chairs. After a brief and uncomfortable interval, it was Hunthar who broke the silence. "Well that is a better explanation as to what happened to them than the one that's been going around!"

Laughter burst forth from the patrons of The Proud Fools Inn, and the people of Herod-Thaar could again reclaim their right to be the proud fools they once were.

Vegtam raised his drinking jack to Hunthar and Leric. "To the future!" he said.

Those within earshot joined in the toast and Vegtam drained his cup. The rest of those who imbibed followed suit. The air of tension that had once held them in thrall dissolved like smoke in the wind. All was well in Herod-Thaar that night.

# ALL WILL BE RIGHTED ON SAMHAIN
# (WITH DAVID C. SMITH)

### PROLOGUE
### REVENGE AGAINST ROME

By 60 CE, the Roman Empire stretches from the deep, black forests of Germany in the north to the rocky deserts of Galilee in the east, from broad fields of wheat and spelt in the south, in North Africa, to the flowery meadows of Britain in the west. In Britain, an uneasy peace exists between the Romans and the Kelts. The Romans have built towns and encampments of stone and wood in the east of Britain, along the English Channel—Camulodunum, a settlement for retired soldiers, and, farther south, Londinium, a commercial center that sits in the marshland of the Thames River. Near Camulodunum lives the tribe of Kelts whom the Romans call the Iceni. Prasutagus, the king of the Iceni Kelts, accepted Roman rule, but upon his death, Nero, the young emperor in Rome, eager to expand the empire he has inherited from the emperor Claudius, his uncle, breaks his agreement with the Iceni and orders all their lands and property to be seized by his governor, Gaius Suetonius Paulinus, who resides in Londinium.

The Iceni Kelts rebel. With their king dead, their complaints are voiced by Queen Boadicea, Prasutagus' proud, fiery-tempered wife. Roman response is swift and unconditional. Suetonius's procurator, Catus Decanius, and his officials strip Boadicea of her throne and governing rights. They rape her daughters, Bunduica and Voadica, in front of her; then Helga, Decanius' amazonian German torturer, publicly whips the former queen, naked, before her people and before the Roman officials and soldiers who have intruded on the village of the Iceni.

Voadica, ill, dies within the year. Boadicea patiently waits until the proper moment to strike back at Rome. At last, Andraste, the great Keltic goddess of victory, promises the queen many bloody sacrifices in her victory over the Roman invaders. Boadicea sends her surviving daughter, Bunduica, to hide in safety with the druids under their leader, Balor, in a

## THE SNAKE-MAN'S BANE

secret sanctuary deep in the forest. Then the Iceni, led by the proud queen, join other local tribes of Britons to move against the Roman occupants.

Camulodunum falls first beneath the swords and knives of the angry Briton tribes of Iceni and Trinovantes. The terrified inhabitants of Camulodunum gather in the temple erected in honor of Claudius to make a stand until help arrives from the IXth Legion. They do not know that Boadicea's army has already ambushed the IXth on the road to Camulodunum and slaughtered the centurions nearly to a man. The Romans in the Claudian temple are also butchered, although Boadicea is disappointed to discover that Catus Decanius and his perverted, whip-wielding German amazon are not among the corpses. The proud Roman and his company have already fled for safety to Gaul. The fearful Governor Suetonius has left, as well; no longer in Londinium, he stays on the move, trying to build a force sufficiently large to confront the inflamed Kelts.

Emboldened by their victory at Londinium, the combined tribes under Boadicea now comb the countryside for Roman and pro-Roman settlements and savage them in bloodbaths, one after another. The Britons are particularly brutal in their revenge at the settlement of Verulamium, home of the traitorous Catavelaunii. Of all the Briton tribes, none was more accommodating to the Romans or more hated by their neighbors than the Catavelaunii. Boadicea's army heaps the carnage high, and the kites and scavengers feast.

Governor Suetonius at last raises an army sufficiently large to withstand the onslaught of the Kelts and makes his stand against Boadicea and the allied Britons southeast of the settlement of Atherstone. The battlefield is not to Boadicea's advantage: she must attack from a wide, open field, whereas the Romans have an entire forest at their backs for protection. But the queen of the Kelts has an army of 200,000; Governor Suetonius's combined Legions II, XIV, and XX comprise only 13,000 men.

Yet Boadicea is confronted by a bad omen. Before each prior attack on her enemy, from Londinium to this field, the queen had released a hare from under her cloak. The hare is a familiar sent from the goddess Andraste. Boadicea had once told Bunduica that Andraste had come to her in a dream and whispered into her ear the secret of divining the outcome of a battle: when the rabbit returns, the Kelts will be victorious. This morning, however, when Boadicea releases the hare, it does not return.

Has Andraste abandoned her?

Those closest to Boadicea hear the queen say, under her breath, "...and if she won't help me, I will destroy them without her." She then mounts the step of her chariot and shakes her spear in the direction of the Romans.

Her wild, waist-length red hair beats in the wind like a mighty flame. Her muscular frame taut, she calls out to her tribes: "See them on the hill with the trees to their backs! Cowards who whip and rape defenseless women! Grown men who sleep with little boys! Let them run to the trees and hide! Have I not shown you the Goddess is on our side? She has sated her thirst on our crimson-stained altars! We have reveled in her name! Let the men of Briton go home even. The women can finish this battle on their own!" In response to her exhortation, the Kelts raise their voices as one and thrust their weapons in the air.

Confronting this display, Suetonius turns his horse and shouts to his men, "Keep close order. When you have thrown your javelins, push forward with the bosses of your shields and swords. Let the dead pile up. Forget about plunder. Win the victory, and it's all yours."

With awful shouts from both sides that rock the sky, the Kelts advance. The Romans hurl javelins, and many Britons drop. The Romans charge in a wedge formation, like a mighty battering ram, crowding in the tribes and going to work on them with short swords and spears designed for fighting in close quarters. The Britons, wielding their otherwise effective long swords, are caught. Before their families, whom the tribes had invited to watch this spectacle, the Britons go down in defeat. Hemmed in by their own wagons at their backs, the tribes are unable to retreat. The Roman cavalry has them flanked on both sides. By the end of the day, the dead lie in tall piles.

Boadicea, having survived the slaughter and aware that her daughter is safe, takes poison that the old druid Balor had given her should she and the tribes confront defeat at last. Forsaken by Andraste just when she most needed the Goddess's strength, the flame-haired queen now is dead and her revolt at an end.

This last battle, however, has driven Suetonius out of his mind. He has become almost more animal than man, drunk with power, enraged at the Kelts, as bloodthirsty as a wolf. His desire is to continue killing and torturing Britons endlessly. Learning of this, Nero sends Julius Classicanius to Britain to replace the rapist Catus Decanius as procurator, and Classicanius sends Governor Suetonious back to Rome so that he will cause no more trouble in Britain.

There has been enough already.

# THE SNAKE-MAN'S BANE

## CHAPTER I

## THE SACRIFICE

A slow wind moaned through the endless forest of tall, great trees. Bending strongly, heavy branches beat together and knocked out an unaccompanied nighttime dirge. The argent moon frowned on the Briton forest, watching like an eye as Bunduica weaved her way among the dark, gnarled boles. In her right hand she carried a torch; under her left arm was a wiggling bundle; slung over her back was a sack that contained fresh water and some few provisions.

Trees began to change, and before the young woman's eyes, as she hurried, the very light of the moon came alive around her. The old druid's mistletoe concoction, which the girl had drunk before entering this heavy forest, was taking effect. Immediately, everything around her burst alive— and Bunduica was walking in two worlds at once.

Here was the forest, ripe with fearful things and the expectancy of the evil to come, and here was the world alongside it, the sinister prelude of the forest and her immediate surroundings—the original world. Here lakes of blood ran in red waterfalls, and men and women took the forms of written characters—ancient runes—and shape-shifted into horse- and boar-headed chimeras. As Bunduica hurried on, one of these boar-headed men, standing now not far away, looked at her and, lifting his right arm, showed her the decapitated head of a man. He threw back his head, exposing freshly blooded fangs, laughed—and vanished, turned into fog.

The inhabitants of this damned world moved like ghosts free to pass through or pass over time. They shifted and dissolved as scenes of aeons came and went instantly, like the dreams of stars, all around the dazed Bunduica. A flaxen-haired woman, bare-chested, with a well-muscled abdomen but only half-human, slithered through the trees, her head and breasts and arms swaying atop her lower body, which was that of a large serpent. Curling and uncurling, the snake woman moved past a long row of impaled torture victims, some of whom yet lived, writhing and sweating, in the starlit mists. Her head swiveled completely around as she examined these bloody trophies; the back of her head, revealed only briefly as it revolved, was the face of a beast that Bunduica could not identify.

The young woman tried to keep her attention focused on her mission. This other world, she understood, was the result of the druidic potion, and she must not allow it to stand in her way or distract her from her purpose. She had suffered much already, but she was strong. Indeed, she looked like a younger version of her mother, the great Boadicea, with her flaming red hair, taut but feminine physique, alabaster skin, and piercing green eyes—eyes full of haunted memories. But Bunduica had her mother's iron will, too, so she walked on through the grim forest with complete determination, as if in a trance.

A crunch of autumn leaves beneath a booted foot not far away reminded her that she was not alone. The two boys, one tow-headed and the other red-haired with freckles and a perpetually sour look on his face, watched her through the trees from a distance. They had been following her for some time. Bunduica was aware of them, but they did not know that. Since ingesting Balor's mistletoe concoction, Bunduica felt as if all of her senses had become heightened to a nearly agonizing level. The boys were undoubtedly following her to spy on her and report back to the Roman officials. Most likely they were of pro-Roman families. It didn't matter. She knew that tonight there would be a reckoning.

She walked past a tree with a leering skull-like face that had been carved by no human hand. The jaw moved as the face tried to whisper to her. As she went by the skullface, Bunduica began to wonder just how far into the forest she would have to travel before she found the place. Suddenly a sharp voice inside her head said, "Look! There it is. To your left!"

Balor's voice, or her mother's? Or her own from deep within her? Bunduica saw a copse of four thick, gnarled old oaks, their tops leaning into each other as if they had grown together in a knot to make a roof. Balor had told Bunduica that when she saw this sign, she would have found the very place where the ritual must be performed.

Now she entered the grove and laid her torch and the writhing bundle on the altar of black stone that sat far beneath the knotted roof. On the sides of this carven block of onyx, strange characters had been chiseled, much like those she had seen in Balor's book. Had this slab of stone really been brought from another world, as old Balor had said? Bunduica shrugged the pack from her back, removed a flask of spring water, and set about quenching her thirst.

She then closed her eyes and made sure that she could recall the rune sounds and words Balor had taught her from his old tome. He called it *The Book of Dead Runes*. This grimoire, written on leaves of strange parchment and bound in skin with clasps of iron and bone, had been ancient even when fabled Valusia, the great kingdom, was young, its first trees green, its skies bright. Balor had given Bunduica the book when he decided at last that the child had nothing to live for but the vengeance she craved. She had spent months begging the blind old man for the occult knowledge she needed to take her revenge.

Balor had said to her, as he made his fateful decision, "You will be working in magick and summoning forces the druids have shunned since before the great cataclysms of old." The powerful magicks within the book were like trickster spirits, he told her; they would likely destroy the user as well as those against whom they were used. He recited the history of *The Dead Runes*. The fierce grimoire had first been in the possession of the race of Serpent-Men, the unhuman creatures that had tried to topple the line of the ancient Great Kings who had reigned before the oceans engulfed Atlantis. It was this race of Serpent-Men, some said, that had bound the book in the age-greyed human flesh that now covered it. Much later, it had been held by a sect of sorcerers in a land far to the east, Stygia. The sorcerers of Stygia had used the book to rule that dusky kingdom; with it, they brought down death and terror on all who opposed them. Even these workers of darkness, however, feared to utter spells contained on certain of the book's leaves. "Stygia long ago collapsed into dust," Balor told Bunduica, "and the book came to be held by two ancient enemy tribes called the Æsir and the Vanir. Through them, it reached my hands. I can tell you that there is a race to the north of the Briton Isles that will one day wash this land in blood, but not in your lifetime. They use written characters similar to those in this book to divine the future, but their runes are a very mild corruption of the dead runes. Some wise person knew what he was doing when he disarmed such knowledge. This will be the last that men will know of the book."

Balor had concluded with a dark warning. "This tome may not even have been born on this earth. Some say that it was brought down from the stars or from another world. What we know, Bunduica, is this: our world sits on top of, or passes through, the world as it truly is, not as it appears to be. For there surely are such other worlds beside ours. Bunduica—when you summon the rune forces, it isn't known whether the dark entities evoked will appear to the human eye, or are invisible demonic entities, or are forces of nature. I myself have not spoken these passages aloud. What I do know, myself, is from the undisputed testimony passed down through druidic tradition since before Atlantis sank. The rune forces are most potent—and utterly dangerous."

And the key to the living forces of the runes, he emphasized, lay in the proper pronunciation and vibration of the sound that each rune represented. "You must practice each patiently. And know that the ritual formula prescribed herein must be followed to the last letter and sound. There is no room for error. Do you understand?"

She had promised him that she did. And now she wished that his ancient strength were here with her. Old Balor, her mentor and foster father since her mother's death, had been wise in the ways of all things.

He had been tortured and his eyes burned out when Suetonius, during the rebellion, had destroyed the druid sanctuary on Mona.

Taking in a deep breath, Bunduica unraveled the blanket. As the cold autumn air hit the baby, he began to cry. Bunduica clenched her teeth and reached for the athame at her belt. The dagger had a black handle that looked as though it could have been fashioned from the same material that the altar was hewn from. She paused as her hand touched that handle, and her green eyes burned with an unholy light. If those who had known her mother could have seen her at this moment, they would have sworn that Bunduica was Boadicea returned.

She began chanting the incantation in a whisper. The sonorous rhythm of the rune sounds lifted above the trees to pierce the silvery moon and grip the sky of the late October night. The sounds grew louder, and louder still. Even in the chill of the cold autumn night, sweat poured down Bunduica's face and drenched her back and her breasts as she intoned the malefic words over and over, calling louder each time. At last her chant built to a crescendo, and she screamed in a language that had never been intended for human organs to resonate: *"Tree-Micalazoda Yom-Gurd! Deesmees! Jeshet! Bonedose! Feduvema! Enttemoss!"* Then, *"Open wide the Gates! Manifest Rune Thorn!"*

Down her fist slammed, driving the dagger into the crying baby's heart. The thrust made a thumping sound like that of a bursting melon. Blood spurted in jets, landing on the surface of the black stone altar. Bunduica wiped a dripping stream of blood from her eyes and grinned. She dipped the fingers of her right hand into the blood and drew the Thorn rune on her forehead, then smiled.

Before her on the darkened slab running with crimson lay her own dead child—the bastard son of Catus Decanius.

## CHAPTER II

## THE HORNED GOD

Bunduica lifted her hands and, in answer to her, the sky split with a crack of thunder that shook the floor of the forest. It was then that she heard the boys break and run.

The people of this land had seen many cruelties and torments visited on human beings, and even for children, such things were common. But the two boys, Tow and Red, had never witnessed such savagery in the context of a ceremony—a ceremony that immediately answered prayers with an earth-shaking retort.

They felt evil coming. They felt it in their bones. They ran screaming in fear of their lives from the blood-spattered witch as rain started to fall in heavy drops.

Bunduica laughed hysterically at them, shouting, "Run, little piggies, *run!*" She snatched the torch from the altar, wheeled with the ritual dagger in her other hand, and gave chase.

The breathless boys now regretted following the young woman, but they had been lost; that was all, and trying to find their way out of the woods. Seeing a woman going into the deep trees alone on this night, of all nights, was an uncommon thing and could mean only mischief. A fellow Briton who was certainly up to no good—the Roman officials would surely pay a nice little reward to them if the boys had just a little more information on this woman.

Just as Bunduica was gaining on the two, she heard a crashing through the trees to her left. Immediately she stopped and, panting, hid herself behind a thick birch. Peering carefully from behind the tree, she saw a hunting party going by. Because her vision was partly obscured by the trees, she only caught a glimpse of the leader of the hunt.

He was a giant. He had long red hair and wore some sort of helmet with horns that dipped and pointed upward. His upper torso was bare and seemed to be inhumanly white although, after he had passed by, Bunduica reflected that the giant's skin might actually have been a funereal greyish-blue. Was he dead? Dying?

Behind him loped a band of hunters with the heads—not of human beings—but of boars and horses and of beasts that Bunduica did not recognize. Most were men, but there were a few women. The strange animals that came behind these hunters, sniffing the ground as they went, looked like giant dogs, but their brilliant red eyes cut through the darkness. These demonic animals, all lean and athirst, made loud panting noises. More of them came then; the hounds seemed to materialize from cracks in the shadows or from the misty air that formed sharp angles and opened suddenly, bringing them forth.

Bunduica herself saw through one of the angled openings only briefly. Close to the opening, just inside it, a goat-legged satyr approached. He was standing inside a scarlet circle that rolled like the rim of a wheel. This rolling circle stopped short just of the opening, and the goat-man pointed a finger at the strange hunting party. He said, "There it is." The abhorrent hound beside him shot out of the angled crack in the atmosphere and joined the hunting party.

The last figure to ride by was a woman with a lizard-like head. She gripped her horse's reins with the clawed pincers of a large crustacean. As she passed by the birch tree, she turned her head with a sly grin, as though knowing that Bunduica was hidden there. Bunduica saw the lizard woman's horse open its mouth in a saber-toothed snarl as the woman's forked tongue flicked in and out of her mouth. They rode on.

Powerful visions, nether-worldly scenes, images from nightmares and dreams. Bunduica judged that these visions were the effects of the shamanistic potion of the druids that Balor had given her. But she now realized that what she had just seen go past was no vision or dream but rather a manifestation in this world, this level of existence, of what she had seen earlier in visions. The visions were as real as she was.

*For there surely are such other worlds beside ours.*

Bunduica recalled the tales told about this one night of the year. Throughout the warm months of spring and summer, the Goddess would walk the earth. It was then that life was given, and all things thrived. Tonight, however, was the night that the Goddess went away. Now the Horned God of the Hunt would rule, for it was the winter of the world, and death incarnate walked the earth tonight, reaping the harvest—the Wild Hunt. Here was the reason why Balor had chosen the night of Samhain for her to call on the force of the Thorn rune in the name of revenge. The angry dead gods, the vengeful spirits and creatures of the other world—this was their night to pass into our world if they could, forcing their way through and taking whatever they might to carry with them when they returned to the dead land of everlasting storms and shadows.

When the Horned God and his party had passed by and were out of sight, Bunduica left her hiding place. She realized that her two young spies were well away from here, probably on their way back to their village with a worthwhile bit of information—which may or may not be believed by the Roman officials. It began to rain hard now, and she decided it were best to be on her way, back to the secret catacombs of the druids, deep underground, where the Romans would never find her again.

After an hour had passed, however, in the deep of the chill night, Bunduica realized that she still had not been able to retrace her steps to the path she had first taken into the forest. Losing her focus by chasing the two spying youngsters had been a foolish act. The rain was now beating down in torrents. She needed to find shelter quickly, but she was unable even to find her way back to the black stone altar, which at least offered the cover of its oaken roof.

Panic was beginning to overtake her. Was she dying? Or had she died somehow already, and was she now between the worlds, or in the world of the Hunt? None, she had been told, who witness the Hunt, its dead gods and its memories and angry spirits, survives to speak of it. Suddenly, the same voice from deep within that had helped her find the altar said, "Look to your left! Shelter!"

Bunduica saw it. There, in the depths of the forest, was a house, all alone. It was a tiny, rustic stone cottage with latticed windows, no two of the same size, and a thatched roof. Vines had climbed all over it, and a stone path before it led straight to a thick oaken door. The door, Bunduica saw through the heavy downpour, was arched and had some sort of hide nailed to it. As she drew nearer, she saw by the light of the crackling sky that the hide resembled the form of a small human being.

If the hide were a warning meant to dissuade visitors, Bunduica was not convinced. She reached the door and lifted a hand to knock on it, but then it opened on its own. Bunduica looked into the single room of the cottage and saw an old woman, a crone as ancient as the trees themselves, stooped before a bright, snapping fire and stirring at a great black cauldron with a large spoon fashioned from a gourd. The woman was dressed in a black cowled robe made from some type of coarse material. Bent as she was, stirring her brew, the old woman turned her head to meet Bunduica's gaze.

"Come in," she said. "I have been expecting company." She then let out a loud laugh, a high cackle, and returned to her work, mumbling about company and chanting under her breath.

Bunduica was fearful but, as in a dream, she eased forward. Behind her, the great oak door fell closed.

Perhaps the wind of the storm had pulled it shut.

## CHAPTER III

## THORN

Bunduica sensed something familiar about the old woman—but what? As she came closer, she recognized that the old woman was working particular spells, turning the ladle around and around, dragging the bottom of the cauldron as though stirring a hearty soup. When Bunduica was sufficiently close to see what was in the great pot, she saw strange skulls floating near the top, bobbing up and down. One head still had strings of flesh on it, although its eyes were hollowed out. One skull was human in shape but displayed the fangs of a vampire. Bunduica could also see the occasional arm swirling in the cauldron's liquid and, as big as the pot was, once thought she even saw a torso lift to the steaming surface and sink again.

The crone again turned her head to Bunduica and said to the young woman, as though she were annoyed at the interruption of her chanting, "The chair on the other side of the table—sit and wait. Soon there will be a rendezvous at the little cottage in the woods." Then she laughed, cackling, as though she had amused herself.

The table and chairs were set against a wall just beyond the witch. Bunduica carefully looked around the cottage as she moved to her seat. The wall opposite the one where the witch worked had an enormous, cobwebbed bookshelf filled with a host of dusty tomes. Bunduica surmised most of them to be grimoires that dealt with the very darkest of the black arts. As Bunduica settled uneasily in the creaking old chair, she tried to look away from the bubbling morass of slimy, green liquid in the witch's cauldron, although she wondered, *Have I created this with Balor's spell? Did I open a gate to welcome this crone into the world?*

To her right was a fireplace. The crackling logs in the grate kept the room moderately warm and also served to illuminate the dim cottage. At each end of the stone mantle of the fireplace was a candle. Each candle was made from the withered left hand of a hanged man and encased in wax. The hand on the farther end of the mantle had a silver ring on each finger. Bunduica saw that the four rings appeared to be identical except each had a different blackened rune engraved on the front of it.

The remainder of the cottage room was dimly lit by candles of various sizes, shapes, and colors. Where it was dark, the darkness in the room was profound and drank the light like a succubus taking her lover's fluids.

Now Bunduica noticed a little girl in one dim corner. She was dirty, wearing a dress made from a sack, and had only whites for eyes. Her mouth had been sewn shut, and her neck craned back so that she could look at the ceiling. But she didn't move at all. She was dead. As Bunduica's eyes adjusted to the gloom, she saw where the girl's head had been severed from the neck and sewn back on. Bunduica wasn't even sure that it was the child's own head because it did seem rather large in proportion to the small body.

Bunduica saw two old broken chairs and others that, although not damaged, were situated in impractical positions for furniture. What things came into the cottage to be seated at such odd angles, leaning against walls or lying on the floor? The wall directly opposite the table where Bunduica sat, on either side of the cottage door, contained more shelves, these lined with the many instruments of witchery. There were a mortar and pestle for crushing herbs, and all sorts of cups and beakers for mixing potions, as well as jars filled with human and animal fetuses embalmed in green liquid that resembled that in the cauldron. Bunduica thought she saw one of the fetuses move, as though it still retained some measure of life. There were dolls on the shelves, both male and female. Most of them looked like actual miniature human beings, and she saw that the heads of all of them had been sewn on. One person had a dog's head in place of a human head; a small figure of a dog kneeled beside him with a human head in place of its own.

The hag turned from her infernal broth and brought a dish of some sort of meat to Bunduica. "Eat!" she commanded the young woman. "This will give you strength!" She set down a large foaming jack of some pleasant-smelling libation and said, "Drink! This will steady you for what is to come."

Bunduica pushed away the dish. She didn't know what was in it, but she could guess. She hauled up the drink, however, and quaffed deeply.

As she set the cup down, the door to the cottage slammed open. Bunduica started at the figure stepping through the arched doorway. It was the giant she had seen earlier, or dreamed that she had seen. He must have been seven *pedes* in height; he had to crouch deeply to make his way inside, he was so tall. His skin was alabaster, startlingly white in contrast with his long, red hair. In shape he looked human, except for his face, which was fixed in a rictus of evil. The curved horns that Bunduica remembered protruded from his head - they dipped toward the ground, and thrust back up in defiance of the heavens. His eyes burned a horrible red. Bunduica couldn't stand to look into them. Two dark bundles hung from his wide belt.

The stranger opened his mouth, showing elongated fangs, and said in a deep, resonating voice, "I don't suppose these two will be troubling you anymore." He reached to his belt and lifted the decapitated heads of the two boys, Tow and Red.

Bunduica almost felt pity for the two young spies.

The demonic stranger tossed their heads onto the floor at her feet. They were nothing more than garbage to him.

Bunduica became dizzy; the room tilted away from her, then toward her, the deep shadows and the candlelight blurring to her vision. Seized in the grip of vertigo, Bunduica tried to look away from the creature's red eyes. They burned. They were awful. She turned to look at the old witch, and saw that the old witch was now gone. But where *could* she have gone?

The horned man came across the floor and sat at the table directly across from Bunduica; the chair was small for him, and she wondered that it hadn't broken beneath his weight. Perhaps it had changed shape in the same way that the witch had disappeared. He asked Bunduica in a booming voice, "Don't like the sight of what you have wrought, woman?"

She summoned the courage to look upon him. Slowly she felt her head begin turning toward him, but against her will. To Bunduica's astonishment, a handsome man with long red hair and a well-groomed beard and mustache now sat across from her. He seemed to have shrunk in size, and horns no longer protruded from his head.

But his eyes were still horrible to look upon. The moment Bunduica looked into them, the red orbs shifted into several pairs of burning slits, and abruptly, a sort of hazy field floated in the air before the creature's eyes. To Bunduica, it looked like a miniature ocean in which demonic eyes awoke and pierced a cosmic veil to penetrate this plane.

She looked away, still facing him, but not staring at those red eyes.

He smiled at her then—and gone were the fangs of the demon. Remarkably, he was now clad in a black silken tunic and breeches fit for a nobleman. He again spoke in a voice that resonated with a more human timbre. "Is this better? We have much to discuss and little time to do so."

Bunduica felt her heart racing and thumping. Her mouth was dry. Trying to speak, in a quavering voice she managed to ask, "W--who are you? What do you want of me?"

"I think it is my place to ask you those questions, woman. It was *you* who summoned *me*."

Bunduica's eyes went wide. "You are the demon sent by the Rune? How—?"

"I *am* the Rune. I am Thorn. I am king of Hel-Valha—and anywhere else I care to tread. The spirit of the child you dispatched to me now screams in agony, awaiting my return. When dawn comes in this world, woman, I must be away to my kingdom. You have offered me a most precious gift with this child you have damned. Now it is I, by my own law, who must give you a gift of vengeance in return. Name your price!"

Bunduica gained strength, then, looking at Thorn, as though he had lent it to her in some fashion, guiding her. She said to him, "This is my price—the torture and death of him who raped and impregnated me, Catus Decanius."

Thorn again took on his original demonic form. From somewhere below Bunduica's line of vision, blocked by the edge of the table, he drew forth a human heart that, she understood, had once belonged to the spying red-haired boy in the woods. In his claw-like grip, he showed it to her and squeezed it. As it dripped blood, the heart formed into a glowing round orb.

Bunduica looked in amazement as a scene inside the glowing ball unfolded before her. Catus Decanius was in his chambers lying in bed. He was not alone. With him were a mother and her son. The mother wore a collar about her throat; attached to it was a leash that hung down one side of her—a leash, as though she were no better than a dog. The boy couldn't have been more than ten years old.

Standing at the edge of the bed, holding her whip, was Helga, the tall muscular German, bare breasted, her bronzed skin glowing. Taken at thirteen from her tribe in a border war with the Romans, unfit for life in a harem and enrolled in the Ludus Magnus, the largest gladiator school in all of Rome, Helga had bought her freedom after much success in the coliseum, then hired herself out as an assassin to any politician willing to meet her price. Hired by Catus, a man with tastes as debased as her own, the amazon was barking orders now at the mother and child as the procurator laughed and squealed with delight, anticipating what he planned to do with the boy, his usual practices.

Helga took hold of the mother's leash and yanked her away, leaving the boy in the company of Catus.

Bunduica looked away in disgust. This was what she had endured when she was raped.

Thorn withdrew the glowing heart and replaced it in a small pouch at his belt. "The worlds have met. I know where he is. Before your sun rises again, Catus Decanius will begin screaming in eternal agony."

"I want to see it."

"You will see it all."

"Then I will come with you?"

"No, Bunduica. You move too slowly. My time is only until daybreak. I must be seated on the throne of Hel-Valha before it is again daylight in this world. But I will return to show you my work before your accurst sun rises. But you — once I have left, wait here inside the cottage. Do not leave for any reason. This is the law."

Thorn departed through the arch of the cottage. The rain had dwindled now to little more than a drizzle.

Bunduica, however, daringly followed behind him, standing just beyond the threshold of the cottage.

Outside, waiting on Thorn, was an enormous horse with the giant, veined wings of a bat and eight legs. Oddly, when Bunduica looked at the eight-legged steed, she saw four men moving beside it, carrying a corpse in a casket. She was reminded of her father's funeral ceremony. He had died leaving half of his kingdom to the emperor, hoping by that generous gesture that the Roman officials would show respect to his family and tribe.

Thorn mounted his great winged steed. It reared on its hind legs and kicked its hooves while flapping the mighty leathern wings. The horse screamed its terrible jubilation to the sky and bared awesome fangs. To be away into the fray of carnage and bloodshed — these excited the beast nearly as much as they did his demonic rider.

Thorn held the fanged, flying beast's reins in one hand and thrust his mighty war hammer, Jolnir, above his head in the other. He screamed the primal war cry that had felled armies and destroyed nations. "Away, Sleipnir," he shouted, and horse and rider soared into the air, mounting the sky of night as though it were a solid road beneath them.

They would fly far to the south, three hundred *millaria*, to the Gallic town of Lugodunon. As Bunduica watched, lightning flashed high above her, and a door with many corridors opened in the sky as Thorn waved his hammer and roared a loud incantation. A door that traversed time and space. He steered the winged beast through the door, and the tear in the sky closed behind them.

Bunduica saw them vanish in the middle of the sky, and she wondered in despair if the demon truly would return. Or perhaps she was indeed dead, now. Or was it that all that she had seen and heard this night had merely been the musings of she herself . . . finally gone mad?

## CHAPTER IV

### REVENGE

Catus Decanius' sleep was fitful. Although he had satisfactorily spent himself in a long evening's debauchery with his slaves and now lay in his comfortable bed, covered with a warm downy blanket to stave off the Gallic autumn chill, something was wrong. His dreams had begun pleasantly enough, with the procurator recalling how he had forced himself on the two daughters of an Iceni noblewoman, taking turns with each before he was spent. His pleasure had been heightened by the fact that their mother was bound, stripped, and alternately whipped and molested by Helga while forced to watch his performance with her daughters. His exhibitionism sent a surge of pleasure coursing through him, and in this pleasant dream, just as Catus was starting to build to another climax, the scene changed.

He was still in his sleeping chambers, but he was in the present, awake. Two burning red eyes looked down on him in the darkness. The head of the horned watcher pushed forward from the darkness. The horrible head hovered in the room and now erupted silently in a flaming inverted star and stared down on the Roman disapprovingly.

Catus mumbled, still certain that he was asleep, "No, no, not me. I was just taking what was mine to take." His bed and blanket were now drenched in his feverish sweat. Finally, he cried out and awoke.

Weeping, he slowly let out a sigh of relief. A bad dream. Perhaps he had overexerted himself tonight. Too much wine.

But as he went to call for a slave to enter and change his sweat-soaked bedclothes, the procurator heard a faint sound. It was the odd noise of someone in the distance beating on a wall. With each strike, the noise

## THE SNAKE-MAN'S BANE

sounded louder and came nearer. Now it was like a giant battering ram, crushing stone and splintering marble.

Catus pushed himself from his bed to investigate, but then paused. The room had abruptly gone quiet—which was shattered by the crashing of a giant war hammer through the wall opposite his bed. Catus fell backward, onto his fine blankets. Another blow—and an alabaster giant with long red hair and jutting horns appeared where the wall had been.

The stranger's terrible face, fixed in a rictus of hate, was the same face Catus had seen inside the hovering, burning pentagram a moment ago in his dreams.

The snow-colored giant bellowed, "It is time, Catus Decanius. I've come to carry you home."

Catus began weeping again and, in fear, wet his comfortable bed. He called for his guards, but no sound came from his throat. Was he still inside a dream?

His sleeping chambers were situated in the middle of the upstairs in the villa. The guards' chambers were off to each end. The two guards on the south end of the hallway slept in the same room, and they were asleep now: Helga had given them the grieving mother slave to play with after she herself was done with her. They heard their procurator's commands, but his voice at first was no more than part of their own dreams.

The giant leaned close. Gripping Catus by the face in his powerful right claw, Thorn dug in until the head dripped blood, then dragged the Roman through the doorway that opened onto the massive hall of the villa.

The hallway was illuminated by torches ensconced at intervals along the walls. Thorn, still holding Catus by the head, slammed him down onto the stone floor of the hallway, pushing him and knocking the breath out of him. Each time the shivering Catus tried to get up, Thorn threw him down again, and each time, bones broke.

Thorn had his back to the first guard who managed to reach the doorway. The delighted giant was watching Catus trying once more to get to his feet despite some freshly broken ribs, a shattered collar bone, and mangled right arm. Thorn leaned with his left hand wrapped around the handle of Jolnir, his war hammer, with his right arm crossed over his left. The head of the hammer rested on the floor.

As the first guard charged in from behind to run Thorn through with his *spatha*, Thorn swung his war hammer up and, without even turning to look, smashed in the soldier's face with a backhanded blow. Bones crunched and teeth and blood flew all over the hallway. The soldier, spinning around, slumped to the stones face first, into a widening pool of his own blood.

A second guard arrived. He hadn't had time to get into his armor, but he had managed to come armed with a shield. He was further armed now with knowledge of his foe, having just seen for himself the deathwork of this giant, truly the most formidable opponent he had yet faced in his service to the procurator.

Thorn slammed a booted foot onto Catus's lower left leg, and more bones crunched. Catus brought up his insides, emptying his guts and doing his best to wipe the remaining vomit from his mouth with his jittery left hand.

Holding the procurator to the floor, Thorn watched the circling guard. Sweat washed down the Roman's face as he tested Thorn's reflexes with a jab toward the abdomen. He moved in several times, feinting, then quickly drew back. The rune was amused, watching this Roman trying to calculate how best to deal with the demonic figure before him.

Then came the wild war cry of the German amazon as she rushed over the top of the stairs at the other end of the hallway.

Moving so quickly that the motion was a blur, Thorn hefted his war hammer and threw it. The great weapon slammed full force into the Roman guard's shield. The force of the blow carried the fighter through the open wall and into Catus' sleeping chamber, the impact breaking his neck and back and crushing his internal organs beneath smashed bones.

The naked, charging Helga fell into a crouch. Thorn crossed his arms and stood as still as a statue, watching her. Quick as a panther, Helga threw three *pugios*, one after another. Thorn quickly caught the leaf-shaped daggers in his left hand. Nostrils flaring, the amazon, dressed only in her weapon belts and scabbards, drew two swords, one with each hand, and spun them in a blinding whirl that cut the air and made whistling sounds as they moved.

The Rune was clearly not as moved by her exhibition with weaponry as he was by her nudity. Whatever else he was, the Rune was male, with instincts for women, and aside from her close-cropped blonde hair, this fighter was an attractive woman. It was apparent that she didn't care for body hair, however; the only hair she tolerated was the little on her head. She was more than six *pedes* tall and was muscular, yet still retained just enough body fat to be appealing in a feminine fashion. Her breasts were large with big nipples, and her skin was well tanned; surely she spent much time naked in the sun. The rune approved.

Thorn's simultaneous indifference to her display of martial skills and clear appreciation of her body infuriated Helga. She snarled, a wild beast. No man had ever stood before her in battle, ogled her bare body, and lived. This demonic figure, whether he were a specter or a man—he would die. His head was that of a demon, but his body was that of a man and would surely bleed like those of all the other men who had had the misfortune of confronting Helga at arms.

By now all ten of the procurator's remaining guards had donned their armor and arrived from the north end of the hall.

Helga hissed at them, "Stay back! He is mine!"

All stopped where they were. Aside from the procurator, Helga largely ran the household; and if the truth were told, every man in the villa feared her as he had never feared any man.

The German shifted her weight onto her right foot, slowly rolling the short swords in front of her. Both swords had been made especially for her. They were each two *pedes* long, the length of a normal *gladius*, but these blades had jagged edges spaced six thumb-lengths, six *unciae*, apart, going all the way down them on both sides. Wielding such blades in battle gave Helga an immense sense of pleasure, as they caused her victim so much more pain than the clean death of a stab wound from the standard *gladius*.

Thorn calmly unfolded his right arm from his left; his mighty war hammer shot back from the crushed guard's corpse in Catus' bed chamber into his fist, seemingly of its own volition.

Helga winced, a look of wonder on her face. Sweat rolled down her body, and her sienna skin glistened as if she had been rubbed down with oil. "Who are you?" she growled. "*What* are you?"

She was used to being answered immediately by anyone within the sound of her voice, but the giant Rune did not react at all. Thorn's silence set her off; as superbly and swiftly as she had ever moved in her fighting life, Helga swung the right-handed sword around for a decapitating blow as the left came up to gut him. No one in the hallway saw Thorn's sword rise, but there it was, in his left hand, deflecting the blow aimed at his neck just as the handle of the massive war hammer knocked aside the German's left-handed sword.

Immediately Thorn lashed out. The head of Jolnir struck Helga in her chest, above her moving breasts, knocking the air from her. Before she could recuperate from that blow, Thorn punched her in the face with his left hand. The German dropped her swords and folded at the waist, staggering backward.

Her nose was broken; the bottom half of her face was red with the running blood. The guards in the hallway stood unmoving then as Thorn retrieved Helga with one hand around her face, lifted her, and tossed her. When she landed farther down the hallway, she rolled headlong down the stairs, out of sight, making a final loud thud as she hit the bottom, then letting out a long moan.

The procurator, seeing this and nearly out of his mind from pain, shouted, "Guards! Fools! Take him!"

Swords slid from their scabbards in the torch light as the score of guards came charging in, shields in front of them. Thorn threw the war hammer into the cluster of men. Howls lifted as men were crushed beneath Jolnir, chests and backs and legs broken apart and heads crushed beyond recognition, as the force of the flying hammer pushed them backwards into walls or caused their own blades to cut them backwards along the throat and face. Thorn held out his left hand; Jolnir returned to his fist; then the Rune drew his sword and waded into the seven Romans left standing.

The first man came charging in with his head down and thrust his sword low in an attempt to disembowel the demonic warrior. Thorn brought Jolnir down on the man's head; the helmet cracked like a nut, and the legionnaire's brains came out and slid down his neck as he dropped. Another Roman stepped forward to thrust his sword, point first, into the giant's heart. Thorn parried the blow with his heavier blade and slit the man's throat with the backhand return.

Two others, wielding daggers, tried to tackle Thorn and drag him down; Thorn laughed as the two thrust the daggers into his sides. These were men well trained in their craft, but their cuts were an annoyance to the Rune, nothing lethal. As the two continued to strike, another guard jumped onto Thorn's back and tried cutting his throat with his *spatha*. Thorn reached back behind him and plucked the man from his back, digging two fingers into the screaming man's eye sockets to get a grip. He lifted the guard over his head and dropped him onto the floor in front of him. The man groaned, eyeless and bleeding to death from the empty sockets. Thorn then grabbed the two digging steel into his sides, gripping them by their heads and slamming them together. Skull and neck bones cracked, and the two dropped strengthless to the floor.

Three remained—one of whom had survived the force of Jolnir's initial blow. Now he was trying to rise. Thorn grinned, stepped over the two corpses on the floor before him, and swung his sword at the guard's heavily muscled neck. In a moment, his head slid from his shoulders and rolled onto the stones, his face locked in an expression of great surprise.

The two Romans left standing now ran for their lives.

Catus, only somewhat lucid, crawled weakly on the floor. Thorn was showing blood down his sides and legs, but already the wounds had closed up and turned to scars, and the scars themselves were vanishing as if he had never been stabbed. The Rune grabbed Catus Decanius by the hair and started dragging him down the stairs. "Your time has come, Procurator."

Regaining consciousness, with a broken nose, smashed left hand, and the multiple cuts and bruises she had suffered from her fall down the stairs, Helga fought to get to her feet. She heard the din of battle and screams coming from upstairs. The demonic stranger was slaughtering everyone in the household. Her ankle was sprained, but she had survived much worse. She hurried away from the stairs, down the corridor, half dragging and half running on her lame foot. *I can be free of this place in a moment*, she told herself. *Rouse the local praetorians. Not even the demon can stand before an army of disciplined Roman steel.*

Ignoring her pain, Helga reached the arched doorway. *The portico. The stables. Then I am free.* She threw the bolt and was through. Outside. Free —

She let out a piercing scream.

There was a flurry of hooves. The two remaining household guards lay one to each side of the doorway, mauled and mutilated. Helga saw the giant, eight-legged horse as it flapped its membranous wings and bared its terrible fangs. She saw its burning red eyes.

Then it was on her.

# CHAPTER V

## YOU ARE THE WITCH

Bunduica had pulled a chair up to the small fireplace to bask in its warmth. She had been drowsing for only a few minutes when the door to the cottage slammed open again.

She was sure she must be dreaming. Could Thorn have returned so soon? Because it could have been no more than half an hour when the Rune had taken to the sky on his flying beast, headed for Gaul.

She came wide awake as Thorn snorted, pushing his way through the opening, and dropped Catus Decanius at her feet. The Roman was bound hand and foot and grimacing in pain from his broken bones and lacerations.

Bunduica stood, looking at her enemy—"*Open wide the Gates! Manifest Rune Thorn!*"—and slowly drew the athame from her belt.

Thorn threw up his hand. "Hold, woman!"

Bunduica stopped close, looking up at him.

"A hunter hunts for food to fill his stomach," said Thorn, "but he does not discard the hide. He needs it to cover himself against the elements in winter. Every death serves many purposes for the hunter. A god is no exception. Know this: It is a god's pleasure to feed on the spirits of human beings. Their lives—every pain, sorrow, and misery—each of these is a delicacy for the god's consumption. A sorcerer possessing the knowledge of a god can do many things."

Thorn walked outside and reached into the saddlebag on Sleipnir. He returned and threw a large book onto the cottage table. It was identical to *The Book of Dead Runes*, the grimoire from which Balor had taught her the runic incantation.

Bunduica was puzzled. "I don't understand. Balor's book?"

"My book," Thorn told her. "It was I who brought it to your world. I wrote it. There are two other copies of it in your world now, but the only one in the possession of a human is the one your druid retains."

Thorn reached down and grabbed Catus Decanius, throwing him hard against the wall so that he was in an upright, seated position. Catus grunted but could do no more. Thorn had gagged him with a strip torn from the procurator's own sleeping robe so that he wouldn't have to endure the annoyance of Catus pleading for his life during the return to the witch's house.

Squatting, Thorn touched his hand to Catus' head and, with an almost pious look on his face, as if in mockery of some sacred religious ritual, he recited an incantation. Catus shook as if he were having a seizure. His face turned purple, and he foamed at the mouth.

Bunduica moved forward one step, then stopped.

As if in response to her apprehension, Thorn told her, "He is not dying. Quite the contrary. Now he cannot die until his body is all gone. Each part of him that you sever will die, but as long as any part of him is left intact, he will feel pain. And so this will go until he is no more."

Thorn grinned as he saw understanding in Bunduica's eyes.

"There is more." The god walked to the fireplace mantle and took one of the silver rings with the rune on it from the wax-covered, withered dead man's hand. He turned and slipped it onto Bunduica's forefinger. Thorn then reached down and with his clawed finger and tore Catus' right eye from the socket. Blood spurted onto the cottage floor as Catus jerked and shook in agony.

"Hold his eye in the hand on which you wear the ring," said the Rune.

Bunduica took Catus Decanius' eye in her hand. As she did, there was a swirling of darkness before her, and a window opened in the midst of the room.

"This ring will help you translate the language in the book. Each severed part of a human's anatomy opens a door by which knowledge may be procured and wonders may be experienced. Do you wonder what is happening and what will become of Catus' henchwoman? Squeeze the eye gently in your hand and look into the window."

A rich, purple-hued pattern pulsated, then exploded inside the strange window. It was replaced by a clear image of Helga lying in a bed. Her eyes were rheumy as she beheld sights not of this world, as if she were dying. Her tanned face had turned a pale, ashen grey. Helga's forehead was beaded with sweat. Two servants of Catus' household now tended to the amazon and wiped the sweat from her fevered brow. Her stomach was swollen as if she would explode. Her feet and legs were tied to the bed, and her mouth was opened in what could only be a scream. Suddenly her stomach exploded and a demonic head burst through.

Blood and offal struck the walls and covered the nearest servant. The servant woman who had been tending the amazon was screaming as she held her hands out and frantically tried to shake the demon's blood from them. Helga, opened from the breastbone down, lay unmoving as everything that had been inside her now lay steaming on either side of her. And still, the demon that had come from her struggled to move from the bed, awkwardly moving itself over her bound legs.

Bunduica had seen Helga die giving birth to a creature with the misshapen head of a monster, the face of a human, and the body of a horse. She saw it as it ran from the mansion of Catus Decanius, screaming its hatred at being born, as its eight horse's legs carried it away into the night.

Thorn then slipped another ring on her middle finger. He drew one of the leaf-shaped daggers that Catus' amazon had thrown at him and grabbed Catus by the wrist. Catus kicked and tried to get away. Tears rolled down his face. Thorn then severed Catus' index finger near the base and squeezed the blood out of it. Catus, kicking and squirming, had vomited from the pain but had been forced to swallow most of it back down because of the gag in his mouth.

Thorn removed a jar of reddish liquid from behind some tubes on the shelf of witches' tools and set it down on the table by the book. He then plopped Catus' severed finger into the jar and told Bunduica, "Soak the index finger in the jar for three days, then dry it by the fire until it withers. Wear it about your neck when you wear this ring on your finger, and no human or animal eye will detect your presence. The rest you may learn of your own accord, as I have provided you with the book and the instruments."

Bunduica held out her hand and gazed wide-eyed in awe at the rings. A smile crept over her face. "Might you destroy the whole Roman army and the Emperor, too?"

Thorn shook his great head. "I am a god of the old world. As I have told you, the new gods feed on the pain, suffering, and sacrifice of human beings. I am an exception. I am the oldest god not to have fallen into oblivion. There is no greater morsel for me than feeding on the very essence of another god. The stronger the god, the greater the hunt, and the greater the feast."

He continued, "It is a new era. Many young gods are being born. There is an upstart god worshipped by a tribe far from here, in the east. This tribe is called the Hebiru. Almost one hundred years ago, the Hebiru god sent forth a son. The god is a war god, but his son preaches peace as a facade to attract and enslave the masses. Over fifty years ago, the Romans put this man to death because of the trouble he caused them. In the years to come, the Romans unknowingly will pave the way for the upstart war god of the Hebiru. Their cult will spread to the far corners of this world. As the faith in this god grows, so shall his strength grow. I will return one day, and I will slay him when the fruit is ripe for the harvest. Then there will be a feast fit for only such a king as myself."

Bunduica remembered Suetonius. "There was a Roman general who was responsible for my mother's death. He took the old druid's sight. They burned his eyes out."

Thorn grunted, whirled, and shoved a clawed hand through Catus' chest. It made a squishy, tearing sound as he quickly withdrew Catus' heart from behind his ribs. Blood sprayed all over the room. Catus, lying on the floor, coughed profusely and gasped as if he were dying. Thorn reassured the girl, "He won't die. He can't until he is all used up." Thorn then squeezed the remaining blood from Catus' heart and held it up to look at it closely. The heart formed into a glowing globe; in it, Thorn saw flashes of battle and wholesale death, and he saw Suetonius' insane glare. The general's face became that of a demonic woman with piercing evil eyes; then it flashed back to Suetonius' grinning leer.

Thorn smiled, a look of pleasant surprise on his face, and he said, "Ashteroth!"

Bunduica cocked her head slightly to one side and gave Thorn an inquisitive look.

The Rune told her, "Your people refer to her as Andraste."

Bunduica's face lit up. "My mother called on Andraste to grant her victory in her war against the Romans. She gave thousands of lives to Andraste on her bloody altars. But when my mother needed her most, this goddess turned her back on her."

Thorn continued gazing into the glowing orb. "Andraste didn't just turn her back on your mother. She clothed herself in the very flesh of the man who destroyed your mother. She now possesses Suetonius."

Bunduica was stunned.

Before she spoke again, Thorn said to her, "Oh, yes! To drink the essence of one of the Ancients again. I am sure that you want to shell the nut that is hiding in that woman. Remember what I said about the hunter and how he wastes nothing valuable? Study the book."

"I am the hunter?"

"You are the hunter, woman. Now…when Catus Decanius is no more than a stump, summon me again. I will take his Ka. That is when the great suffering shall begin."

"His Ka?"

"The Ka is the spirit that leaves the body once it truly dies. Once I have his Ka, I will sever it into seven layers, the Ka still existing, but in turn branching off into the Ren, Sekhem, Akh, Bau, Sheut, and Sekhu. Each will suffer its individual torments but, at the same time, each will bear the pain of the others, as well as feel all of the suffering at once again, as a whole. Study well *The Book of Dead Runes*. With the ring and the finger charm, you may come and go between this cottage at the edge of the world and the world of men."

Bunduica asked him then, the Rune, Thorn, this strange man or godman whom she had, with Balor's magic, called down to exact her revenge on Rome, "Tell me… am I dead?"

"Dead?" he said to her.

She had spoken the runes, sounding the syllables perfectly. Under fear of the storm and the wild hunters, she had hurried to this witch's cottage— whoever or whatever the witch had been. She had feared then that she had died and was only her spirit, whatever remained of herself. What had Balor said to her? *You will be working in magick and summoning forces the druids have shunned since before the great cataclysms of old.*

Thorn, sensing her concern or reading her mind, said to her in a voice now more pleasant or soothing, "No, Bunduica, you are not dead. Through your courage, you have earned your place. Here you may stay. *You* are the witch you first met here. Although this place borders on space and time, your accurst sun still rises here, and so I must be away. Know that I will return in four months, as you reckon time, on the eve of Brigid, in the heart of winter."

And he was gone.

All of it — storm, boys, book, babe, hunters, witch, bloody vengeance — a dream, a dark dream, no more than that?

Feeling the strength that Thorn had left her with, Bunduica slowly turned and glared at the mutilated but yet living figure lying on the floor. She smiled, and the smile rose to her eyes and imbued them with a maddened glint.

She went to Catus and removed his gag.

He vomited everything within onto the cottage floor. Then he screamed, and he screamed, and he screamed. And that was just the beginning of eternity as he was to know it.

## CHAPTER VI

## FEEDING ON THE ESSENCE

## OF ANOTHER GOD....

In a far corner of the throne room in the great palace of Hel-Valha, the Ka of Suetonius Paulinus was stretched out on the floor and was skinless. His flesh had been neatly peeled away from his body and was now spread out and fastened to the floor by hooks made of fire. He could still feel the pain of suffering that torture. He—his Ka—was held in place by vine-like tendrils with suction cups that sent a burning serum coursing throughout him. His sightless eyes stared, as though keeping them open might somehow grant him some sign of light. He opened his mouth and screamed repeatedly, but no one present could hear him.

In fact, no one anywhere could hear him aside from himself. The sound that escaped his throat was silent to those outside his own head but amplified infinitely inside him. The deafening roar of his screaming served only to heighten his pain and confusion, but the actual physical pain to his Ka was such that he could not cease, and he could not die.

His Sheut was nailed to the wall with daggers. His Sheut was himself, precisely similar to his body as it had been on earth, but it was a complete shadow of that body from head to toe. The hilt of each dagger was an elongated reptilian head that bit him over and over, and his body shook in convulsions, wracked with venomous pain. His head leaned forward, and from his mouth drooled spittle. The falling drool was the shadow of spittle as it hit the floor and vanished as though it had never existed. Suetonius' Ka felt the venom coursing through his veins, felt himself dying the death that he could never partake of. His Sheut, in turn, felt the acid boiling through the veins of the shadow; heard the deafening screams amplified infinite times over. Each of the seven aspects of his being was isolated in separate viewing chambers by invisible barriers, and each felt the pain of the other, and all felt the torment collectively.

The Ka of Catus Decanius was in another far right corner of the throne room. Catus slowly slid down the spear he was impaled upon as it rose out of the floor in an endless upward motion. It was the Spear of Endless Ascent. Blood ran out of his mouth, and he moaned. His arms had been removed, and his legs were now in their place. His arms were where his legs had been, and he wore his internal organs on the outside of his body—intestines, heart, liver. His Ren, which was his true name, stared into the Mirror of Truth at his own jackal head and wept in shame. He couldn't stop weeping at the revelation of what he truly was and always would be.

He wanted to try to find a place to hide, perhaps to curl up, to become a child again, but he was frozen in front of the magick mirror, and always would be.

To all of this Thorn gave no heed as he lolled on his throne. The throne was carved of solid onyx, and the top corner posts were adorned by the ancient horned skulls of his ancestors set into the onyx. On each skull sat the two ravens, Hugin and Munin. They took many forms and flew throughout all the worlds and dimensions, gathering whatever information Thorn required.

At the Rune's feet, gorgeous women of all shades writhed in an orgy of unending pleasure. There were goddesses and succubi of all types intertwined. Some looked like mortal women, some were snow white and had red eyes like Thorn, and some had wings and were covered in thin fur, as are bats. There were sirens with the bodies of mermaids and mouths of fangs, and there were those who were mortal in form but colored like various jewels. Transparent beasts, lions, apes, and man-sized lizards casually loped in and out of the throne room. They looked as if they were made of crystal.

Thorn slumped on his throne in the ecstasy of the greatest intoxication a god can experience. The smoking pipe that now lay on the arm of the onyx throne gave out the remaining mists of what was left over from the previous session of his feeding. Rubbery vine-like tubes ran from the pipe and were fastened with suction cups along the body of Andraste.

Andraste was securely fastened by multi-colored, jewel-like bands to a stake that rose from the floor. She writhed and burned in a fire that sent out waves of flames in all colors, some visible to the human eye, many outside the range of what humans recognize. The burning goddess was contained in an invisible, cylindrical barrier, penetrated by the suction-like, flexible tubes attached to Thorn's pipe. Her screams, like those of Catus Decanius and Suetonius Paulinus, could be heard only inside her being, infinitely amplified as they were.

Thorn was taking her very essence into him, and this act had left him in a slumber, within the Great Dreams that only an Ancient can hope to dream. The Rune was intoxicated by all seven layers of the goddess' spirit, and he would revel in the visions and dreams that were the wondrous events actually taking place on another plane. When this euphoria was complete, he would awaken ten times stronger than he had been before taking up his pipe.

Even now, the light was diminishing in Andraste's piercing, evil eyes as the fire consumed her. As she burned, she shifted and changed into the various incarnations she had assumed down through the ages, from the demonic appearance of the platinum-haired, terrible goddess of victory down to the dark-headed, full-bosomed peasant girl she had assumed to waylay hapless men and drag them down to their doom. Only a few more burnings remained before Thorn would consume her essence, before Andraste fell into oblivion and become as if she had never been.

Thorn smiled the smile of an Ancient in the throes of the Ecstasy of the Great Feast.

## EPILOGUE

Bunduica's prowess in the black arts had grown so rapidly and to such an astonishing degree that it had surprised even Thorn. Upon the Witchmaker's last visit to his prodigy at the cottage at the edge of the world, Thorn had concluded his stay with, "I don't think you will be needing me for anything else."

She had thanked the Rune and wished him well on his next hunt.

Occasionally Bunduica would look in on old Balor. The old man swelled with equal parts pride and awe each time he heard the voice of the woman that he considered the daughter he had never had.

Aside from visiting the old druid, the witch's trips into the world of men became less and less frequent as her strength in her art had grown. She much preferred the company of succubi, incubi, lamiae and the associations with assorted other-worldly creatures at the celebration of the sabbat.

With the overwhelming number of feats that she had rapidly been capable of performing, it had only recently dawned on Bunduica what results the practice of necromancy might yield.

---

Just a shadow of a woman was cast on the faintly candlelit wall of the cottage on Beltane. The shade spoke in a waning voice like one who is dreaming aloud. "You have done well by your tribe. You have avenged the Iceni, and you have avenged your kin. I will always love you."

Tears rolled down Bunduica's face as she sobbed. "I will always love *you*, Mother."

Faint, and fading back into the world of shades, Boadicea trailed off. "I... know..."

...Leaving Bunduica alone in the empty room.

In the distance, she heard the ecstatic cries of the demons, devils, nymphs, and satyrs reveling in the sabbat, her new home.

# THE HEART OF THE BETRAYER

## CHAPTER I

## THE HERO AND THE WOLF

The clangor of steel on steel resounded across the battlefield. A few remaining villagers crossed swords with a handful of invaders as three of the local men gathered around a large wolf that was tearing a man's throat out on the ground. Man after man had fallen before the wolf. Before any of the beast's victims could strike a blow with their swords and spears, the monster had darted out of their midst and back in, hitting one man like a lightning bolt before jumping on another and savaging his face. One of the fallen man's eyes was torn out of its socket and lying on the ground as he held his hand to his bloody face and screamed in agony. The next man struck at the wolf with his sword, but the creature was already behind him, crushing the back of the villager's head with its powerful jaws. The man's brains oozed out onto the ground. The last villager to face the beast realized that this was no ordinary wolf, while he watched the monster stand on its back legs like a man, towering over him as it snarled its razor-sharp fangs into a rictus—casting its cruel arrogant gaze on the horrified villager. Before the man could raise his spear, the monster leapt, dragging his human foe down to his death on the cold earth.

Argantyr was surrounded by four warriors. His long black hair and lengthy beard were speckled with blood, and his steel sinews rippled as he stepped into a fighting stance, holding his large broadsword in both hands. His emerald eyes sparkled, and he grinned as the first man rushed in and brought his blade up and down at Argantyr's head. Argantyr blocked the blow with his sword and made a quick arc with his blade, coming back around to slit the man's throat. Another foe moved in quickly, thinking that he would have time to sink his dagger into Argantyr's ribs while he was regaining his balance from the blow he had just dealt. Argantyr's blade came through and cut down his adversary with the return. A third man came in with a short axe, but Argantyr was on him and cut him down before the man knew what was happening. The blade made a thumping sound as it sliced through the man's abdomen, and his innards spilled on the ground.

There was a loud growling as a bear-of-a-man came into Argantyr's view. Argantyr gritted his teeth and braced himself as the giant came wading through the dead bodies of his enemies. The large man's braided beard and square-cut brown mane were caked with the blood of those who had the misfortune to step into the path of his battle-axe as it had wheeled and spun out the fates of Argantyr's falling comrades. The man stood at least a whole head taller than Argantyr. A deep booming command issued forth from the bellowing giant, "Tell your companions that Ursas sent you to join them in Hel!"

Argantyr barely ducked the blow of the giant's axe in time and heard the whistling of the steel as it went over the top of his head. Ursas was deceptively fast for a man nearly the size of a bear, but Argantyr moved at twice the speed of the giant and drove upward with his sword into the man's guts while he used his left hand to cut the big man's throat with his long dagger. This man was defending his village, but Argantyr had killed men for as long as he could remember. The remaining villagers fell before the swords and axes of the marauders. The battle was over.

Where the huge supernatural wolf had been, there now stood a man with a grizzled red beard and a shock of dirty tangled hair. His head was cocked to the left, and his icy-blue eyes were void of sanity while he leaned on his axe and stared into cosmic vistas undreamt of by anyone save the fey—those touched by the twisted and unclean things that rule the outer gulfs. His mouth, mocking human flesh, formed into a lopsided grin. Foam gushed from his mouth. He wore the hide of an oversized wolf like a cape on his back. The skin of the beast's head and its ears came up and fit over his head like a cap. The man's name was Klak, but those who followed him called him "the Wolf." He was the leader of the band of marauders who had just taken the city of Horan. Horan was like so many other settlements in the far western corner of Gorn, barely ruled by feuding nobles, since Gorn had been torn apart by civil war. Horan was like all of the rest—a ripe fruit for the plucking for a marauding band of seasoned fighters made up of murderers, criminals and sell-swords like Argantyr.

Argantyr's companions who yet lived gathered round him and fell behind him. Since Argantyr had joined the Wolf's band of marauders, he had quickly earned their respect, not only by his skills in battle but by the amount of wine and ale he could imbibe, his skills at gambling with dice, and his ability to wench all night and fell his foes like chaff before the sickle the next day.

The men had their backs turned to Klak as they bragged about how many men they had killed to each other. Klak heard one man say loudly, "…and Argantyr slew that tree-of-a-man like Donar felling an Ice Giant."

Klak wrinkled his nose and spat. "This will all change when I reach

Aroon-Joon," he mumbled.

---

The scene before the sorceress receded as she drew back from the glowing green scrying orb in which she had just viewed the battle where Klak and his mercenaries had taken Horan. A beast-like sound of heavy breathing issued from behind her. She spoke to the horned figure who sat languorously in the darkness, "Soon we shall have the Talisman, my love." She looked to be no more than a maiden, but her deeply resonating, husky voice and confident mien betrayed her years. "Soon you shall taste the essence of gods and the souls of men again, and you will revel in the bloodshed of war. Know this thing and persevere, Witchmaker!"

## CHAPTER II

## CONSPIRACY

Klak handed the crying infant to Tharat as the wizard told Klak, "You will need to get this powder into his wine cup. It will turn the bravest champion into a cowering cur." Tharat held up the vial of white powder for Klak to see. "He won't be able to lay a hand on a weapon without emptying his stomach and groveling before you." The old wizard had thin white hair, and his filmy blue eyes shifted when he talked. He looked at Klak and snapped his teeth. His right eye was larger than the other and looked off to the far right. He was wearing a dirty brown robe and his tiny, sharp teeth were white as ivory. "This thing will not be easy. The problem will be getting the powder in his cup without him noticing." The dirty little wizard snapped his teeth again after speaking.

Klak glared at Tharat, his voice becoming deeper as he told the little man, "You will stop snapping your teeth at me like an old fox getting ready to go into a hen house if you value your life, wizard!" Klak knew that Tharat ate human flesh, but he didn't care. Klak himself had consumed the flesh of another human being on several occasions when he was changed into the werewolf but had no taste for it when he went about on two legs as a man. He would have long ago dispatched the corrupt little wizard to Hel had it not been for Tharat's usefulness as a dealer in magickal items and potions that truly worked. The dirty little man fell silent, fearing the Wolf's ire.

Klak broke the silence. "I don't care to hear your rambling, wizard. I have already taken care of arrangements to get Argantyr to drink the powder." Klak made a cruel barking sound as he laughed. "His woman is a sloe-eyed slut we took in a raid to the Far East. She is called Arju-Lao. He hasn't wenched a night since we took her. He tried to set her free, but she wouldn't go. He thinks that he saved her from me and my men taking her and doing what we want with her, but when Argantyr is deep in slumber or away, she comes to my sleeping quarters and asks me to do as I like. She likes to be treated rough. Once Argantyr is out of the way, I will give her a good beating and put some cuts and bruises on her. She told me how much she likes it. If that fool only knew! He trusts her. She will have no problem getting him to drink the powder." Klak barked out another laugh. "Once I am shed of Argantyr, I might even brand Arju-Lao and keep her around for a while."

Tharat's eyes shifted nervously, and his tongue lashed out and licked around his mouth. "You know that if you take her while you are changed to the Wolf, she will be like the others? Her body torn and mangled—her…"

Klak's glare penetrated into the deep recesses of Tharat's brain—those pre-human levels that control the survival mechanism. There was a long pause as the Wolf's eyes burned through Tharat.

Uncomfortable, Tharat changed the direction of the conversation. "Be careful, Wolf. I have seen visions of a battle between a wolf and a great demon that grows out of a man—a demon of such a magnitude as I have never seen before. This man who spawns the demon is…"

Klak growled, "Here is the rest of your payment, wizard!" The Wolf threw the sack of gold coins to the ground at Tharat's feet and wrenched the stoppered vial containing the powder from the wizard's hand, nearly knocking the little man down.

---

As Klak rode back to the nobleman's home that he had taken as a temporary residence—a part of the spoils of his growing band of mercenaries' war on Horan—he stopped to look out over some ancient ruins. He felt a chill go up his spine as he recalled old legends of a cruel wizard's imprisonment and torture of an elephant-headed god from beyond the stars. The particular wasteland that Klak looked upon was supposedly the site where a great warrior had destroyed the wizard and, in turn, crumbled his weird spiraling tower to dust. This was said to have been a part of Aroon-Joon when it was called Zamora—in times long past. Klak spat and mumbled to himself, "Legends… it probably never happened." He rode on, but Klak was uneasy all the way back to Horan.

Argantyr and the rest of Klak's men sat around the table at their wine cups and foaming jacks of ale. They were in the dining room of the manor that the Wolf and his men had appropriated from the now deceased Count Dagnus, whose decapitated head rested on a spear in front of the house. Arju-Lao carried a cup filled with wine to Argantyr. As she passed Klak, the Wolf told her, "Make sure that Argantyr drinks it!"

A mirthless grin spread across her face as she said, "Assuredly, sire. He has already imbibed one cup containing the powder. This will be the second." Her almond eyes gleamed an inhumane light. The Wolf reflected her gaze with his own leer and smiled at her assiduousness.

Argantyr didn't seem to notice Arju-Lao or anyone else in the room as the exotic beauty set the fresh cup of wine on the table before him. He was deep in thought—*spiraling back down a path he had forgotten in his youth—admiring a butterfly as it landed on a flower—the sweet smell of spring and a joyous occasion around a campfire with his family—a gift of fruit from a little girl who was his dear friend in times fell to dust—just like her frail body had returned to the dust when the sickness had taken her. A tear rolled down Argantyr's cheek—what was wrong with him? He had forgotten how to cry long ago—even before he had killed his first man.*

Arju-Lao told Argantyr, "Drink, my love! Celebrate victory once again! You have earned it. You all have earned it."

Arju-Lao's words brought Argantyr out of his trance, but he still felt much remorse for what he had lost—and what he had become.

Argantyr picked up the cup and stared into it. The Wolf was watching him. At first Klak thought that Argantyr knew the wine was tainted and this made him uneasy. Argantyr was like a lion in battle. Klak had watched the man surrounded by foes, cutting them down like blades of grass before they could even close in on him. Argantyr had saved the Wolf's life twice. Once when Klak's attacker was poised to run him through from behind with cold steel—Argantyr had stopped the man in his tracks with an axe thrown to the head. Another time, the Wolf had been wounded and fallen to his knees. A Gornian chieftain gripped Klak by the hair and had his knife on his throat—when Argantyr had rushed in at the last moment and toppled the chieftain's head from his body with a single stroke of his sword. Argantyr was a formidable foe, and Klak was uncertain about his ability to best Argantyr unless Klak was changed into the werewolf—even then Argantyr might not be so easily vanquished. This way was better; it would show to all that even Argantyr would cower before the mighty Wolf.

Klak breathed a sigh of relief when Argantyr tilted the wine cup to his mouth and started on his second glass of ensorcelled wine. The Wolf had had only a few drinks of wine, but was feigning drunkenness. Arju-Lao moved over close to Klak. Argantyr had nearly finished his second glass of wine when Klak wrenched his sword from its scabbard and bellowed out into the feasting hall for all to hear. "Any man who can best me at arms can have all of the plunder taken from the raid on Horan yesterday!"

The Wolf looked around the room at the men as they cast their glances down at their cups or upon other parts of the room. A few of them shot quick glances at Argantyr, but he seemed to be deep in his own thoughts and to not hear Klak's challenge.

Klak shouted out louder a second time. "I said, 'Anyone who can best me at arms can take the spoils from yesterday!'" He reached over and roughly pulled Arju-Lao to him, adding, "I will even give you this whore to play with!" making sure that Argantyr saw him squeeze Arju-Lao's left breast hard with his right hand. Argantyr snapped out of his trance. His limbs would barely move. His hand went to his sword hilt, but he fell upon the floor. Argantyr tried to rise and felt his stomach churning. He vomited the wine up on the floor. The Wolf roared with laughter. He went over to where Argantyr was lying prostrate on the floor, trying in vain to lift himself up. Klak squatted beside Argantyr. He drew Argantyr's own sword from his scabbard and put it in his hand saying, "Take your sword and fight, champion, or your woman will be servicing your fellow dogs tonight... and me. It's not as if I haven't had her already."

Arju-Lao burst into bell-like, high-pitched laughter. "Argantyr knows how to take a man's life on the battlefield, but he has no idea about how to take a woman in bed." A few of Klak's men laughed at her jest, but most remained silent.

Arju-Lao told Argantyr, "Why don't you take your sword and face Klak? I always suspected you were really a coward. A woman wants to be taken by a real man, not made love to by a timid sheep." Arju-Lao pulled Argantyr's head up by his hair and spit in his face.

The Wolf nodded his head in Argantyr's direction as the fallen warrior was still struggling to rise from the floor. Most of Klak's men went over and started beating Argantyr. The few who straggled behind just watched. Most of these men were hardened at birth. Some of them were from tribes who cast newborn babies into embankments of snow to prove that they were worthy of life. Some of them were orphans who had grown up in the streets of cities such as Tulanarth and Taktreer, doing whatever they had to do to survive. If they hadn't been shaped into what they now were as children, life would have made them murderers and cut-throats somewhere along the way.

When the men were finally finished beating Argantyr, Wintaun drew his sword and looked to Klak for his approval. Wintaun had always resented Argantyr for his martial prowess and his luck with the women. The Wolf's face split into a horrible grin as he shook his head and said, "No. Dump him in the ruins on the outskirts of Aroon-Joon where they say it is haunted; in the place they called the city of Zamora in ages long past. He can bleed to death there, or let the devils that haunt the place have him. You dogs worked him over pretty well. Not even Argantyr could survive such a beating. Likely, he'll die before you get him there. Either way, we won't be seeing the cur again."

The men picked Argantyr up and made for the door of the manor. Arju-Lao walked over and leaned back against Klak. The Wolf put his arms around her as they grinned like hyenas at the broken and bloody body of the dying man leaving their sight.

## CHAPTER III

### RESCUED BY THE WITCH

Argantyr opened his eyes. Everything was blurry. He heard a woman speaking. "You are fortunate to be alive. If I hadn't found you when I did, you would most certainly be dead." Her voice was deep and resonating, but feminine, nonetheless.

Argantyr choked out, "Where am I? I need to…"

The woman's voice fell to a soft whisper like a mother comforting her child, "Shhh… What you need is rest… Then you can tell me."

The woman laid her cool hand on Argantyr's forehead; when she did so, his sight receded into darkness. As he fell off into slumber he mumbled, "I need to kill the Wolf… need to kill…"

The woman said, "All in good time. You need rest now."

Dreams assailed Argantyr like an invading army. *He crouched within himself like a child hiding in the cool forest while murderers and rapists rained terror down on peaceful villagers with fire and sword. As he receded into himself like a fetus in its mother's womb, he felt the spring breeze touch his face and savored the aroma of the honeysuckles and lilacs in bloom. The earth was a living, breathing entity again; and Argantyr was glad to be a part of this wonderful sentient being. He saw his parents waving to him as he made his way to the forest. He heard his mother call to him, "Be back by supper!" His father was gathering branches for the* bonfire they would have that night.

The severed tree limb in the forest became his sword as he pretended to slay Ice Giants and imagined the tales that would be told of his valor in Cruach's feasting hall that evening. Of a sudden, there came the rumble of horses' hooves. Argantyr heard the curses of men without gods or souls as they crashed through the forest close by. Argantyr ducked behind some trees into the fort that he had recently constructed of branches with newly grown green leaves.

He heard the shouting of the village men as the steel entered their guts and cut their throats and the cries of the women as they were defiled. He thought that he heard little Bessa screaming. Argantyr shook with rage and fear and tried to withdraw further into himself as he lay there hidden in the trees. A man came riding back his way—one of the marauders. He looked directly into the tree limbs where Argantyr was hiding. The man knew he was there. Argantyr looked out through a space between the limbs. When he did, he saw the man glaring directly into his eyes. The man was Argantyr—Argantyr himself. Argantyr, killer of men.

Argantyr the man woke up screaming. His fever had broken. He managed to stumble out of the bed and reach for a sword that had been lying by his bedside. When he picked up the sword, a shock ran through his body that knocked him sprawling onto the floor. He tried to raise himself up but could not. The mysterious woman was kneeling by his side, helping him back into the bed.

She told him, "You are getting stronger; soon, you will be ready."

"Ready for what?" he inquired.

"Ready for what you have to do. Vengeance burns in your heart. I can see it surrounding you."

"The Wolf—I have to kill him."

"I know," she said as her piercing green eyes bored into him. He noticed what a beautiful woman had been caring for him. She was petite and had long wavy red hair. Her body was taut and muscular, and her low-cut dress revealed the top of her ample bosom. In spite of her athletic build, she was beautifully feminine in every respect.

As she looked into his very being, she spoke as if she were far away. "My heart once burned for vengeance too. And I got it. The men who had destroyed my life, destroyed my sister and my mother. The men all died. I had the satisfaction of seeing them suffer. I helped them suffer, and suffer they did—endlessly. My mother fought them for a while. She raised a great army. But their army was greater. She made them pay in blood, but finally they defeated her; and she took her own life."

The woman spoke as though she were entranced. "Then I called Him—the Rune—Thorn, the Witchmaker. The one before whom no man or army can stand."

Her face snarled into a rictus, and her green eyes blazed—a hellish emerald fire. Her sultry voice rumbled, and she growled like a demonic priestess singing praises to a patron devil. "Not even the mightiest of gods can vanquish him, for he feeds on their very essence!"

"What is your name, woman?"

"My name is Bunduica," she said, seeming to become aware of her surroundings again. "But all of that of which I told you happened in ages long past or yet to come. I have travelled through time so much that I am not sure when it was."

"I am Argantyr. I was once a killer of men, but now I cannot bring myself to pick up a sword."

"I know this, but you will be able to kill again. You have lain in a fever dream for weeks now. We had best lay plans for you to exact your revenge and destroy those who tried to kill you."

"Why are you helping me?"

"We… I have been watching you for a while, Argantyr."

"Watching me?" Argantyr asked, experiencing a feeling of unease at the woman's answer.

Bunduica turned and picked up a round object that immediately blazed into a glowing green luminescence. She held the glowing orb before Argantyr and said, "Look! Even now you can see your former comrades and their werewolf chieftain."

Scenes quickly played out before Argantyr's eyes—scenes of wholesale rapine and murder. Klak and his men took another city—then another—then another. More women and children screamed. More men died. Klak's army rapidly grew and swelled with each city that fell along the way. The marauders sat at the table of a recently appropriated villa and Arju-Lao bounced on Klak's lap as he and his men laughed in drunken revelry.

Bunduica made a gesture and moved her hand over the top of the orb and the light was extinguished.

Argantyr still stared at the scrying orb in amazement. "Arju-Lao yet lives?" he wondered aloud, doubting what he had seen.

"Aye. That is one more reason why we need to quickly set things into motion. The Talisman that I need is still in the werewolf's possession." Bunduica poured some liquid into a cup. "Drink this while I explain to you all that is involved."

## CHAPTER IV

## THORN'S ARMOR

Argantyr and Bunduica walked along outside. It was night time, but the skies were a dim red instead of black; Argantyr could still see quite well. Trees whispered to one another and walked around on their roots—the roots lashing themselves into the ground when a tree stopped in a new position. Bunduica told him, "Do not fear the Irminsuls. They will not harm you." This was a strange world that Argantyr had found himself in since he had awoken from the fever dream. He wondered aloud if he were dead, but Bunduica assured him, "No, you are not—and soon you shall be more alive than you have ever before been."

Bunduica led Argantyr deep into the hilly forest, to the mouth of a cave. As they stood before the yawning cavern, Bunduica told him, "Inside you will find it—the suit of armor that will make you invincible. The mightiest army will not be able to defeat you."

"But how am I to fight when I can't even pick up a sword?" asked Argantyr.

"You shall be as a monstrous war machine to anyone who stands in your path—man, god, or demon. I shall go in with you and show you, but you must don the armor and experience Thorn's power—alone. Your being must merge with the essence of the Rune to regain what you have lost—and then some. You shall see through the eyes of Thorn. As he passes some of his strength to you, so you will pass some of your strength as a living being to him."

"'Thorn?' You have told me of Thorn before, but I still don't fully understand what or who it is that you speak of."

"I told you that long ago I delved deeply into the blackest of arts to gain the knowledge to destroy those who murdered my family and outraged me." Argantyr nodded. "The old druid Balor was my mentor," Bunduica continued. "He was like a grandfather to me. He presented me with *The Book of Dead Runes*, the most powerful book of magick on the earth or any other world that I know. After much study and connecting with the runes in the book, I summoned the Thorn rune. I did not know what to expect. But a mighty warrior king came. He was larger than a man and had hair the color of freshly spilled blood, while his skin was white as snow. He is what some would call a demon. Call him what you will, but he is the physical manifestation of the Thorn rune, as well as he is the Rune itself. Thorn told me that he would destroy the Romans, and he did. But we tarry too long; come inside and see for yourself!"

Bunduica entered the mouth of the cave, and Argantyr followed. As they entered the cave, Bunduica took a torch from a bracket in the wall. She held her hand over the top of the stick, and it burst into flames. Argantyr could see written characters on the walls. Argantyr nodded his head. They looked similar to those used by the priests of the Æsir and Vanir—warlike races that dwelled across the sea and to the far north of his Tuathic people.

The cave was dank and smelled of earth, even though Argantyr wasn't sure that they had entered the earth that he knew. They went through a large chamber that contained doors to several smaller chambers. Bunduica pointed to the doorway of the far left antechamber, and they passed through it. There were life-sized figures displayed there. As Argantyr looked at a snake-man, Bunduica explained that these were trophies of Thorn's many hunts and battles. They walked on. Argantyr marveled at the regal skeleton of a large man sitting on a throne clutching a mighty broadsword. Bunduica told Argantyr, "He was a great Atlantean king, whom Thorn had admired. Thorn keeps his skeleton and Hel-forged sword here to honor the warrior king."

Argantyr gazed upon the jewel-encrusted crown of the great king. *Those jewels would buy a kingdom in this age.*

They walked on past a silver-winged minotaur and stopped in front of a suit of armor. Argantyr estimated that the armor was nearly seven feet in height. He wondered how he was to move in armor of such girth and stature as his eyes took in the details of the eldritch suit. The whole suit was of a shiny black color and looked as if it were made of polished stone. There were runes all over the armor—they appeared as though they were etched into the suit. The helmet would cover the skull and had eye holes and a cheek guard. The suit of armor seemed to stand there of its own volition—sentient. The helmet rested on top with nothing visible to support it other than a black void.

Bunduica spoke. "I must now leave you. Come back to the house—to the spot that I showed you near the black stone. There you and Thorn will find Æbbath. You… Thorn will know what to do." With these words, she turned and made her way out of the cave.

As Argantyr buckled on the last piece of armor and slipped the helmet over his head, he felt an incredible surge of power starting at the top of his head and moving down into his forehead, through his throat, through the heart region, into his groin, down to his feet, and then into the ground. He felt heat moving through his body; then at the base of his spine, he felt the power spiraling back up toward the base of his skull. When it reached his head, he heard strange music as he had never before experienced. The agony and the ecstasy of the experience brought him to his knees.

Glimpses of another life flashed before him. *He was wading knee deep through snake-men as he hacked and slayed his way to a destination he didn't remember. A naked barbarian queen screamed behind him as the snake-men clutched at her to take her away to their breeding camps. Long daggers shot out of Argantyr's gauntlets. He spun around and threw a dagger with each hand as one found its way into the heart of one snake-man; the other blade went into the second reptilian's throat. Argantyr quickly turned to face a snake-man rushing upon him with a battle-axe. He hacked into the monster's belly with his mighty broadsword and the greenish-yellow reptilian ichor sprayed into the air before him and spattered his armor.*

Argantyr could feel his body changing. He was growing in both girth and stature. He tried to rise to his feet, but screamed in agony and fell to his knees again as horns sprouted from his head—horns that curved down and jutted back up in defiance of the heavens. His hair turned red as blood and grew even longer to fall down over his swollen, rippling muscles. Argantyr rose to his feet, standing nearly seven feet tall. The suit of armor had all melded together forming one piece. As Argantyr looked down and flexed the mighty sinews of his arm, he saw that the armor had molded itself to fit his body like a second skin. Argantyr grinned a razor-sharp smile, baring the elongated fangs in realization of what he had become—he had now merged and become one with the Rune—Thorn; God—Demon—Witch Maker—King and Warlord of a strange empire that existed in ages undreamt of by man. Time was merely relative. Thorn had been here before man, and he would exist long after man was no more.

More visions came to Argantyr: *Beings with long triangular heads formed of opaque crystal surrounded Argantyr—Thorn. The beings were cloaked in white robes and they ordered Argantyr to kneel before a god made of white light sitting upon a throne before him. Argantyr heard himself laugh; gruff booming laughter that sounded as if it issued from the throats of ten hellhounds. A host of tendrils shot out of Thorn's weirdling armor and penetrated the light-god's very core, draining it of its essence as the temple dimmed to darkness and started crumbling around him.* Argantyr realized that these memories belonged to Thorn and that both he and Thorn were now two entities sharing one physical body. Argantyr could feel Thorn's thirst for sustenance as the Rune sensed Argantyr's yearning for vengeance, and Thorn answered him, "We give strength to one another. I will grant you vengeance, and you will, in turn, bring me the Talisman that will give me life in this domain—for I have stayed far too long here and am beginning to fade. Once you have faced your greatest adversary, and we have the Talisman, our bargain will be complete." They turned and left the cave.

## CHAPTER V

## THE BATTLE COMMENCES

Æbbath burst forth from the ground. The colossal creature's skin looked as though it were cut from a polished red ruby. Its membranous wings spread as dirt and rocks exploded into the air and trees were uprooted. Thorn charged in and jumped on the creature's back, getting a hold of its horns, and then shifting his grip to the reins. The beast flicked its forked oily black tongue out of its mouth like a serpent. Argantyr knew that Bunduica had made arrangements for their swift travel, as Klak's ever-growing army was rapidly marching hundreds of miles to the north of Aroon-Joon; but Argantyr hadn't known the specific means of travel that she had planned for Thorn and Argantyr. Thorn shouted commands as Æbbath took to the skies with the armored giant on the back of the Hel-born creature. Maybe Bunduica thought Argantyr would fear Æbbath, but at that moment Argantyr heard his own cry of jubilation issue forth from Thorn as the Rune threw his head back and roared Argantyr's battle cry—the battle cry that Argantyr thought that he himself would never raise again. Thorn and Argantyr raced out on the winds of dusk on the back of Æbbath as the beast dipped its elongated neck and screeched its own awful shout to mimic that of its rider.

---

"Do you think that I am pretty?" Arju-Lao taunted the girl in the cage. The prisoner did not respond to Arju-Lao's question, though she understood what her tormentor had asked her. The caged girl had yellow hair that had been made much lighter by the sun since her days in captivity. The prisoner couldn't have been more than thirteen years old.

Arju-Lao's face split into a sinister grin, and her dark almond eyes pierced through the girl. "When we get you out of this cage, you will talk plenty once the Wolf squeezes those firm little breasts of yours hard and fills you up with his manhood. I think that will be more than you can take; and I am going to help him."

The girl's heart pounded, and she felt as hopeless as the rest of the prisoners who had survived Klak's last few raids. The Wolf had heard that the auction blocks in Quan-Kara would pay nicely for young female slaves, and these unfortunates who were in Klak's captivity were bound for a life of servitude to the cruel, wealthy merchants and nobles of the city. The young men who yet lived were made to march along behind the cages. The males were used for labor until the whole army had reached the city—there, the prisoners would be put to the sword once they had served their purpose.

Tarac had been taken in the raid with his younger sister, Taren. He was a few years older than the yellow-haired girl, whom Arju-Lao took much pleasure in tormenting. The heat and long days of marching had finally taken its toll on Tarac and he dropped to the ground. A soldier immediately kicked the fallen boy and yelled, "Get up!"

Taren gripped the bars of the cage so hard her knuckles turned white as she cried, "Tarac!"

Arju-Lao laughed, "You do know how to speak, slave girl."

One of Klak's men rode his horse to the back of the line and told the mercenary who was kicking Tarac, "Go ahead and cut his throat. Klak says his sister should see this, so that she will learn how to behave, if she knows what is good for her."

The soldier reached down and pulled Tarac up by his hair. Taren was in tears and screaming hysterically. As the mercenary brought the long knife up to the boy's throat, a demonic screech issued from the sky; and the monster swept down into the ranks of Klak's men. The men scattered, taken by surprise. The armored demon riding the winged creature swung his battle-axe and severed heads from the bodies of several men while Æbbath sped through the host of Klak's army. Æbbath and the rider were again borne aloft while the soldiers fell back. "Archers, forward!" Klak ordered. "The rest of you, fall back! Bring the beast down and hack it to pieces with your swords and axes! I want that rider taken alive! He is to be made a hymnar; he is to be shorn of his arms, legs; his tongue cut out. I will carry the torso in a box to show men what happens to those who dare to defy Klak, the Wolf!"

No sooner had Klak made his boasts than the beast plunged downward again. The bowmen let loose with their volleys, but the creature quickly flew upward and out of the reach of the arrows and then rapidly plummeted again, landing to the rear of Klak's army. Thorn leapt from the beast's back and crouched down, one knee touching the earth. He pressed the palms of his armored hands on the ground, and flames exploded from where his hands touched the earth and raced out into the ranks of Klak's army. The men screamed in torment and rolled on the ground in an effort to extinguish the fires that singed their flesh and burned them to death. Wagons burned, and the men were in disarray. Thorn was already among the soldiers—hacking and slaying with his battle-axe. His axe whirred and whistled, singing its song of slaughter; and Æbbath took to the skies with a man in his clutches as the soldier's sword and helmet fell to the earth.

A mercenary met Thorn with an axe. Thorn leaned back as he heard the

## THE SNAKE-MAN'S BANE

wind whistle off of his adversary's weapon. The Rune immediately retaliated by bringing his own battle-axe over his head and splitting the man's skull. His enemy's helmet was shattered in twain, and blood spurted up as the man's brains seeped out onto the ground. The runes embedded in Thorn's armor glowed with a hellish red luminosity as he felled foe after foe with his battle-axe.

Thorn was like a lion surrounded by packs of hyenas. His axe moved so fast that it was a shining silver blur of death. One mercenary managed to get in and ram his sword into Thorn's back, but the sword vanished when it was pulled through the eldritch armor and disappeared into another dimension. Thorn bashed the man's head in with the butt of his axe handle and roared with laughter. A few soldiers were able to briefly move in and strike a blow here and there while their comrades died. Those who managed to use their swords in an effort to penetrate Thorn's armor realized too late that no weapon could bite into the strange suit.

Argantyr remarked to Thorn, "It is easier making war than I had remembered."

Thorn snorted, "The real struggle is ahead. To completely break the curse that was placed on you, you must fight Klak alone."

"Fight the Wolf alone?" Argantyr exclaimed in wonder.

"No... Not the Wolf. Klak!" Thorn growled. "The spell preventing you from fighting is temporarily broken, and you are gaining some of your strength back. The potion closed off corridors in your brain that allow your skills in combat to surface. As long as you are in this suit and joined with me, those doorways are open. Do you remember what I told you about how we lend strength to each other?"

The voice that was Argantyr inside of Thorn's body answered, "You told me that we are joined together by this suit of armor, and that we give each other strength."

More blood splattered on the polished jet-black jewel-like surface of the fantastic armor, and the runes etched deep into the armor glowed as red as the freshly-spilled blood. Thorn grunted while he finished splitting one of Klak's men down the torso, "Indeed, I told you that we lend strength to one another; but that is not all—the bargain must be finished by you obtaining the Talisman that will rejuvenate me, and you alone facing the man responsible for your binding, to finish breaking the spell of the potion."

"But I am in a weakened condition outside of the armor, and Klak is more than a man. He is a werewolf!"

Thorn growled, "He won't be for much longer!" as he quickly swung his battle-axe twice, decapitating the two men facing him. They were still holding their swords as their heads landed on the ground with a resounding thump.

Thorn had smote and heaped the bodies high as he waded through the dead mercenaries that had made up the Wolf's shattered army. The remainder had fled; so had Klak's prisoners who had once been bound for the auction block in Quan-Kara and a life of bitter servitude at the hands of cruel and perverse masters. All that was left were the dead and the dying, aside from a lone figure that stood leaning on the hilt of his great scabbarded broadsword across the smoking battlefield from Thorn. The man had tangled hair and a red beard, and he wore a large wolf skin that covered his back like a cape with the beast's head draping over his own head. Klak and Thorn were separated by only a few stacks of dead bodies. The stench of charred flesh, freshly-butchered human meat, and death itself were overpowering.

"*Who* are you? *What* are you?" Klak asked as he looked at Thorn with both a sense of hatred and wonder.

Joined together as they were inside of the suit of armor, Thorn could feel Argantyr's tension mounting as Argantyr hissed through clenched teeth, "Be careful—the werewolf!"

Thorn responded to Argantyr's unease by turning the head of his battle-axe to the ground and leaning on the handle. Thorn's face split into a hateful grin, and he growled in a voice that sounded like ten angry men speaking in unison, "I am Thorn, and I deliver your death to you, Wolf!"

Klak's face wrinkled and moved uncontrollably, a look of uncertainty spreading across his countenance.

Thorn continued, "You do remember the man who saved your life on more than one occasion? The man who you thanked for his service by stealing his woman and trying to kill him."

Klak looked away from Thorn's gaze. *Even with all of the evil that Klak had perpetuated, nothing could begin to approach the horror and agonizing insanity that he knew that he would experience if he looked into those burning red eyes. They held both that which is too good and that which is too evil for man and those two elements combined and created its own entity that entwined and swam in an eternal lake that was the beginning and the end.*

Klak shouted, "It wasn't me that wanted Argantyr gone! It was that slant-eyed whore that took up with us when we took Jade-Chuan-Kune!" Klak was biting down hard on his lower lip and mumbling something between his words to Thorn. "She wanted us—all of us to use her, and use her rough; but Argantyr was in the way!" Klak was frothing at the mouth as he mumbled something again in a language that was not intended for the human tongue.

"Incantations! This is how he does it—changes. I have seen it many times!" Argantyr put in hastily.

Thorn showed no concern for action as Klak burst into laughter and went on, "There she is now! Argantyr can have her back! You can take her to him, demon!" Arju-Lao sprang from behind an overturned wagon and started to run.

"Should we not stop her?" Argantyr asked of Thorn.

Thorn calmly answered, "There will be time for that later, Argantyr. You are getting ready to fight a battle, and the prize is you get to reclaim your manhood."

The change came on fast when the snout burst forth from Klak's face and his body quickly covered in hair as he bared razor fangs and ascended in height. He had much experience at quickly changing to the giant wolf on the battlefield and the transformation, once it started, had only taken seconds. The werewolf snarled and sprang at Thorn. Thorn quickly stepped to one side and tossed the Wolf to the ground. The werewolf rolled over and came up, baying its awful war cry, which Argantyr had heard many times just as a battle was brought to a close.

The werewolf leapt onto Thorn and tried to get its claws into the Rune's throat. Thorn picked the Wolf up by one powerful claw of his own—the Rune's mighty sinews flexing inside of the armored sleeve that clung to him like a second skin. Thorn slammed the supernatural beast onto its back and growled, "I could end this now, Wolf; but I made a deal and there is another who must see to your death."

The Wolf leapt to his feet and stood up on his hind legs. Argantyr thought he saw a cruel and arrogant expression that looked like a smile. Argantyr braced himself for the attack inside of Thorn's body, but before the werewolf could leap, tendrils shot forth from varying points in Thorn's armor and penetrated the heart, throat, forehead, stomach, and groin areas of the creature. Thorn breathed deeply as he absorbed the very essence of the beast. The werewolf was being drained of its vital energies as Argantyr watched the coruscating colors: reds, blues, yellows, and greens, which were the very physical manifestations of the Wolf's essence that were riding Thorn's breath as he inhaled the energy into himself.

Thorn remarked approvingly, "A substantial morsel—for a minor god. Klak used the enscorcelled werewolf's skin to invoke one of the Fenrir and become a werewolf—a manifestation of the Wolf God who devours worlds when they have come to their end. Except now he is the one being devoured. All that is left on your enemy's back is the mangy hide of a dead animal now."

Klak was kneeling on the ground breathing deeply. Thorn took one last deep breath as Klak, who was once called the Wolf, collapsed on the ground. Thorn removed the scabbarded sword from his side and let it fall to the ground as he said, "Reclaim what you have lost, Argantyr, and don't forget your part of the bargain." Thorn then stepped forward and left Argantyr standing alone. The armored Rune and Argantyr were again two separate beings, and Thorn was nowhere to be seen. Darkness assailed Argantyr as he collapsed on the ground a few feet away from where Klak lay.

## CHAPTER VI

## ONE MAN MUST DIE!

A booted foot to the ribs nearly brought Klak off the ground as Argantyr growled, "Get up and meet your death, Wolf that is a wolf no more." Argantyr had regained consciousness several moments erenow and was waiting on Klak to stand and draw his sword.

Klak coughed and a wicked grin spread across his face. He found his feet and barked, "Give me space, dog!"

Argantyr stepped back, drew his sword, and with a sweep of the blade, indicated that Klak now had space to prepare himself for combat.

---

Dusk was rapidly approaching under the greying sky while steel clashed on steel and curses and oaths were exchanged between the two men. Argantyr cautiously circled Klak. Though he was no longer able to change into the great supernatural wolf, Klak was still a deadly swordsman and as formidable a foe as any Argantyr had faced on a battlefield. As the two men circled and parried, Argantyr caught a glimpse of Arju-Lao watching the combat between the two swordsmen. She quickly ducked her head behind a charred wagon that had been used to hold prisoners. The distraction of Arju-Lao nearly cost Argantyr his life as his sword came up at the last moment and stopped Klak's sword from cutting his throat; the impact of Klak's blade cut Argantyr's face instead. Argantyr paid no heed to the wound that Klak had just dealt him; he had been scarred by countless such savage fights as this one. The two men winced as they strained iron sinews and, steel on steel, pushed away from each other. Klak came in again and aimed a disemboweling thrust at Argantyr's lower torso. Argantyr managed to turn to the side as Klak's sword raked his ribs. Argantyr could feel the blood trickling and mixing with his sweat.

Argantyr's strength ebbed while visions of his past life flooded into his brain: *His parents and friends gathered around a bonfire—singing—*

someone made a jest—laughter—running through the grassy fields with his best friend, Bessa; she was a beautiful little girl—they were only months apart in age.

Klak moved in and swung his sword at Argantyr's head; Argantyr brought his sword up and deflected the blow as he arced back around and stabbed into Klak's thigh with the tip of his blade on the return. Klak's leg buckled.

More visions from Argantyr's past: *A village left in smoking ruins. Argantyr was now an orphan; he looked upon his mother's and father's funeral pyres. His father had fought valiantly, but there were too many of them. His mother had taken her own life rather than be defiled like the rest of the women of his village. He saw little Bessa lying on a bed coughing as the fever took her after what the men had done to her.* Argantyr gritted his teeth and, as spittle flew from his mouth, he shouted, "No more! I buried you all! I buried you and myself with you!"

Argantyr sprang like a tiger and rained blow after blow of steel so fast that the stunned Klak barely managed to counter his enemy's assault in time. Argantyr's head momentarily filled with visions of his family and tribesmen growing dim as they waved to him from the bank by the creek where his home had been in what was another life. He shook his head and dealt blow after blow, each one faster than the previous attack. Klak was gasping for breath and bleeding heavily, but Argantyr had never felt as alive as he now did—the blood pumping through the iron sinews that gripped his steel. Klak tried one last desperate attempt; marshalling all of the strength left in his battered body, he struck a quick blow at Argantyr's head but was still far too slow for the panther-like reflexes of his adversary as Argantyr stepped back and brought his own broadsword down on Klak's weapon, breaking Klak's blade in twain. Argantyr wasted no time in bringing his sword back through and slitting Klak's torso open. Blood frothed from Klak's mouth as he dropped to his knees and looked up at Argantyr. Argantyr kicked the hilt and shard of broken steel jutting out of it towards Klak and growled at the man, "Pick it up! Pick it up and fight, *Wolf*!"

Klak held onto his stomach in an effort to prevent his innards from tumbling out onto the ground as Argantyr bitterly stated, "It wasn't so long ago that I was on the ground due to you and your concubine's treachery. I at least gave you a chance to fight. It appears as though the Norns have woven out the final thread of your wyrd, Klak." As soon as Argantyr spoke the last word his sword flashed in a deadly silver arc that sent Klak's head flying from his shoulders and rolling on the ground.

Klak's dead face looked up from the ground in horror. Arju-Lao ran and dropped at Argantyr's feet, clutching at the man's legs, groveling and crying, pleading with him. "The terrible things they made me do. They hurt me so badly! They told me they would kill you if I didn't go along with Klak's plan. That is the only reason I did it! Argantyr! You have to believe me. I could love only you. Tell me you believe me! Tell me, Argantyr!"

Argantyr breathed deeply and clenched his jaw; he squinted—eyes full of pain. He looked down at the girl groveling before him and helped her get to her feet. Arju-Lao wrapped her arms around Argantyr, and he slowly raised his arms to return the embrace. She clung to him tightly for several moments. Finally Argantyr whispered to Arju-Lao, "We must be gone now."

"But where will we go?" Arju-Lao asked, realizing for the first time that the course her life had been on had changed significantly.

Argantyr responded, "I need to go see some… friends. I have to complete a bargain I made."

Arju-Lao looked all around the smoking battlefield. The wagons had all burned and all of the horses that were left living had long ago fled. She said, "It will take several days on foot to reach civilization. How far away is our destination?"

Argantyr was watching the sky. Arju-Lao cast her gaze aloft and saw what Argantyr had been staring at: a horned and winged creature bathed in the light of the moon. The thing's appearance reminded her of the stories in her homeland of the legendary dragons of Jade-Chuan-Kune.

"Traveling on foot won't be necessary," Argantyr said quietly. He waved his sword in the air, threw back his head and shouted, "Ho! Æbbath!" The flying beast acknowledged Argantyr's call by dipping its head and plummeting earthward.

## CHAPTER VII

### THE SINISTER TALISMAN

Arju-Lao was seated across from Argantyr in the candlelit dining room, watching him savagely tear into the roasted boar as he grabbed a loaf of freshly baked bread with his other hand. He had not eaten anything in two days, and he was famished. Arju-Lao delicately pecked at a plateful of roasted potatoes and vegetables cooked in herbs. The dish reminded her of the food of her homeland, but in place of the rice, there had been potatoes.

Their hostess had been absent only briefly when she returned to the dining table with a glass of red wine and set it before Arju-Lao. Still chewing a mouthful of the roasted boar, Argantyr burst out enthusiastically, "This is Bunduica's special wine that I told you about, Arju-Lao! The best in these parts! Fit for a princess!"

Arju-Lao forced a smile at Bunduica seated on the end of the table. Arju-Lao didn't like the way Bunduica's cat-like eyes shone like fiery green emeralds, cutting through her as though she could see every secret of her soul and was privy to every wicked thing Arju-Lao had ever done. Arju-Lao noticed that there were four plates set at the dinner table, but only she, Argantyr, and Bunduica were present. Arju-Lao's almond eyes squinted, looking as though they were nearly closed. "Bunduica, where is this other person who is to dine with us?" she asked.

Bunduica responded in a voice as smooth as silk, "Oh, he is out hunting. He is a hunter."

"What does he hunt?"

"Gods," Bunduica answered with a wry smile.

Arju-Lao pretended to giggle like a young girl at Bunduica's jest. "He-he! Gods!" There was an uncomfortable moment of silence as Arju-Lao's feigned laughter stopped as quickly as it had started.

Bunduica's gaze shifted to Argantyr's eyes and back to her own wine cup when suddenly Argantyr boomed, "You haven't tried the excellent wine yet, *my love*." The words almost choked Argantyr to say and prompted him to empty his own vessel and put it back down. Bunduica lifted her cup and thrust it forth, silently toasting Arju-Lao. Arju-Lao wrinkled her tiny nose at the sanguinary liquid and quaffed deeply, half-emptying the cup in one drink. The wine immediately went to Arju-Lao's head. It had a sweet taste going down, like a burning amalgamation of chocolate, caramel, and liquid flowers. Made uncomfortable by the silence, she finished draining the cup as an excuse to ask Bunduica for some more, just to get the woman to leave the room. No sooner had Arju-Lao brought her wine cup back down and set it on the table than her head followed the vessel to the table with a thump as the young woman became unconscious and her brain swam in a sea of primordial darkness.

---

*A blast of light becoming a single source of illumination in the darkness that was before the beginning—and would be there when all had ended... The light was a sun shining in the night that radiated rays of runic shapes from its core.*

The light receded and became smaller as the woman drew back with her candle from where Arju-Lao lay on the cold black stone altar. Arju-Lao could hear voices. *But where was she? The last thing she remembered was dining with Argantyr and his friend, Bunduica... and the wine. The wine! She had been drugged.*

As if they could both sense her realization of what had happened, Bunduica laughed and Argantyr said, "I guess this makes us almost even now, Arju-Lao. You put powder in my wine, and now we have put powder in your wine. Though, I don't think that you are going to be faring as well as I have in the aftermath."

Arju-Lao tried to move, but her limbs were bound by red vines—supernatural tendrils that were much stronger than she was. She tried to let out a scream, but her mouth held a gag to prevent any sound from issuing forth.

Bunduica gruffly chuckled, saying, "I would have liked to have heard you, Arju-Lao—it is exciting—but your *lover* told me how he loathes to hear a woman scream. He said it brings back bad memories of when he was a child."

Arju-Lao tried again to move her limbs, but her resilience availed her not, for she was much too firmly bound.

Bunduica had placed a pillow under Arju-Lao's head so the woman could witness what they were doing in the room. For the first time, she noticed the demon in the darkness. His skin was alabaster, and his long hair was red as blood. His large muscular frame lolled on the ebon throne he sat, and he breathed laboriously. Something was wrong with him. He was the one on the battlefield. The one who destroyed Klak's army and brought Argantyr to kill her true lover, the Wolf.

Tears welled up in the girl's dark almond-shaped eyes and she began to tremble with fear as her brain tried to correlate all that had happened and simultaneously started to speculate on what was happening at that moment.

As if in answer to the questions that raced through Arju-Lao's head, Bunduica broke the silence. "Yes, Arju-Lao, Thorn is the demon who destroyed Klak's army. With help from Argantyr, of course. Thorn has stayed too long in this world that we inhabit tonight. He is weak. The synchronicity of Thorn and Argantyr in Thorn's suit of armor lent strength to both men temporarily. The curse that you helped Klak put on Argantyr is now completely broken, but I made a deal with Argantyr, and there is one last thing he needs to do to fulfill our bargain."

Arju-Lao strained at her bonds on the altar as tears rolled down her face onto the cold black stone beneath her.

Bunduica continued, speaking as if she were in a dream, "Once... ages ago, I was the daughter of a proud queen. Her name was Bodicea. My father had died and left Bodicea as the ruler of a wild race of warriors known as the Iceni. There was a mighty empire to the east called Rome. Even before my father Prasutagus had died, there had existed, at best, an uneasy peace between the Iceni and the Romans. One day, the Romans came... They came and took away my mother's governing rights. They tied her up and whipped her. Made us, me and my sister Voadica, watch while they did it."

Bunduica had raised her voice to a crescendo, and her piercing emerald eyes gleamed with madness. Arju-Lao's heart was pounding as though it could burst from her chest at any moment.

Bunduica looked at the floor and fell silent for a moment. Lowering her voice, she regained her composure and turned her head to the side and continued, "They raped me and my sister. Both of us. Over and over again. My sister, Voadica, died shortly thereafter; but I survived on the hatred in my heart alone... I went to the deepest, darkest recesses of my mind, and I opened up corridors that, it is said, no human being should open. One night, I made the ultimate sacrifice that a mother can make. I sacrificed my own son in a ritual, and Thorn came. Thorn came, and he destroyed all of those who'd had a hand in our downfall; and he made them suffer; and O they did suffer for aeons! But he didn't stop there; he knew that I loved him like I could never love a man, and he took pity on a poor broken girl whose only reason to live was the vengeance in her heart—and now that that was sated... what was left? I will tell you! He taught me the secrets of black arts that no wizard on this earth knows. He showed me wonders that no other human eyes have looked upon. But now he is weak and dying, because he has spent so much time with me here, in the House on the Edge of Time, and has been long absent from his kingdom of Hel-Valha. He needs the sustenance to open doors that only he can open and return himself home; and the last object that I need for the spell is in you; and it has to come out!"

Bunduica drew a long dagger and, holding it flat in both hands, offered it to Argantyr. The dagger was etched deeply with runes like those on Thorn's armor. Bunduica cast her penetrating gaze upon Argantyr and said, "It is time to fulfill your part of the bargain."

Bunduica raised her arms and chanted, "*U-u-ur! U-u-ur! Come forth from the Land of Castles where the towers spiral into forever and timelesstime where time and space have no meaning. Come forth, cause of all causes. Origin of all creation. Origin of immortality! Origin of all law and of chaos. And origin of all vibration in which the great secrets of truth abide! Come forth, thou ghosts of the Runestorm, and heal the one who is stricken with torment and fading into the darkness that was here before time and surely will be here when time is no more. For he is of your essence, though he manifests in matter. U-u-ur! U-u-ur!*"

Argantyr stood over Arju-Lao, both hands clutching the hilt of the long rune dagger as Bunduica's incantations heightened to a fevered pitch.

Arju-Lao saw weird angles opening and tumbling in the air all around her and she screamed into the cloth that muffled her cries. Bunduica shouted, *"Tree-Micalazoda Yom-Gurd! Ho-dag nona nu nak no! Deesmees! Jeshet! Bonedose! Feduvema! Enttemoss! Open wide the Gates! Manifest Ur!"* Bunduica screamed as loud as she could, "Now, Argantyr! Bring forth the Talisman! Do it now!" Argantyr drove the dagger down with all of his might into Arju-Lao's breast. Blood jetted up, and the angled openings in the air about the room shot forth a glowing green light that coalesced and was absorbed by the rune dagger. Argantyr gritted his teeth and shifted the blade of the dagger around, deep in the dying woman's chest. He then reached into her bloody breast and pulled out her heart—still beating due to Bunduica's sorcery. Argantyr turned and handed Arju-Lao's heart to Bunduica, saying, "Our deal is finished, witch woman. You now have your Talisman."

Argantyr watched as Bunduica walked over to the demon sitting on his throne—dying. As Bunduica held up the Talisman, she said to Thorn, "Here, my love, the still-beating Heart of the Betrayer torn from her breast by the one whom she betrayed; the Talisman needed to restore you to life so that you can open the corridors leading back to Hel-Valha."

Bunduica put her arm around Thorn and held the heart up to him, slowly feeding him the delicacy, a treacherous and evil heart sustained by sorcery, the sinister Talisman that gave him life.

## CHAPTER VIII

## ROAD OF THE LONE WOLF

The four soldiers sat at their foaming jacks and wine cups around a table at the Wolfshead Inn. It was a crowded tavern in Horan, being one of two that hadn't been burned to the ground in recent years. One of the men at the table slapped Taren on her behind and gripped it as he chuckled through rotten teeth. "How much for a night's pleasure, serving girl?" he inquired. The man sitting next to him laughed at the girl's silence.

The innkeeper saw Tarac's face turn red and knew the boy seethed with rage at the expression of fear and humiliation on his younger sister's countenance. As the young man reached for the knife at his hip, the portly, balding barkeep shot Tarac a disapproving glance. "Not if you want to keep your job—or your life," he said. "I gave you two a place to stay and the means to make an honest wage when you came here begging for food and shelter, and telling your story about being taken in a raid on your village, but I sense trouble, and I would wager that the two of you are hiding from the authorities somewhere. If you are going to live in this city, then you are going to have to obey the laws of this city. I see no harm in charging a small fee for them to sleep with her. We could split the pay, say, sixty-forty. That would be sixty percent for me and forty percent for you and your sister—split between the two of you, of course."

An old one-eye sitting at the table of the soldiers chortled with a phlegmy drawl. "Now, hold on, barkeep. Who said anything about money? You know what you just told them youngsters about obeying the law. Well, we *are* the law; and *we* say what is right here."

Another man sitting nearby spoke. "If we knew you was going to be selling those kinds of sweets, we would have done had our turn with her, barkeep. I'll offer you good money for that."

Suddenly, a man who had been sitting in the corner for some time listening to the conversation got up and walked over to Tarac and his sister. "I have a better deal for both of you than any of these pigs can offer you." He placed two sacks of jewels on the bar and nodded to the two siblings. "Go ahead, take them and leave this pig-sty. You can buy ten dung heaps like this one with one of what is in that sack."

The whole room fell silent as Taren looked at the man and picked up the bag; her brother followed her example. The man who had given the jewels to the youths was an imposing figure, dressed in black accoutrements fit for a nobleman and wearing knee-high leather boots, silk breeches, a shirt of fine dyed wool, and a cape of black silk lined with red. He gestured toward the door of the tavern and solemnly commanded Taren and his sister, "Now, get out, and don't come back here."

As the two siblings exited the tavern, the old one-eye sitting at the door was the first to break the silence. "Who are you that comes in here and interferes with the law, dog? Your neck could be in a noose as soon as I say it."

Without turning to look at the man the stranger replied, "There has been no law here since Count Dagnus' head was set on a spear in front of his house in Horan, and Klak and his men sat feasting at Dagnus' table; and even at that, there wasn't much law before then. The whims of a few cutthroats do not concern me any more than I value their lives."

The one-eye nodded to the other three men at the table. The room exploded as the soldiers' table was overturned and flashing swords came out of their scabbards while the barkeep ducked behind the counter. The first man to rush forward caught a dagger in his chest. As the stranger drew his sword, he threw his cape over the next soldier rushing him while his steel met another mercenary's sword and came back around and slit the man's throat. He threw another dagger into rotten-teeth's thigh, and the wounded man dropped to the floor as the soldier with the cape over his face worked free; but it was too late for the man, as the stranger drove his cold steel into the man's guts and the mercenary dropped to the floor—blood gushing from his mouth, and his intestines spilling out onto the floor.

Rotten-teeth tried to rise, but the stranger's broadsword hacked at the man's neck, and his head rolled on the floor, face leering upward in a black-tooth grimace. The fight had been over as soon as it had started.

The stranger looked behind the bar at the cringing barkeep and laid two small jewels on the bar. "Use this to pay for the damage and get some real whores around this place so the sellswords will stop trying to rut with children."

The stranger then walked out the door of the Wolfshead Inn to where his horse was tethered in front of the tavern. As he prepared to mount the great white steed, a young girl's voice cried to him, "Wait, sire! Where are you bound? We have no home, nor way to travel." It was Taren.

The stranger answered, "I am bound for Tuatha, where I hail from; but first, I have business on the outskirts of Aroon-Joon. You can follow me until we get to Arthing; then we must go our separate ways. Take the horses that belonged to the soldiers; they have no need of them now. Mount quickly and let us be gone before more soldiers come."

Tarac and his sister mounted the mercenaries' steeds. "What is your name, man?"

"My name is Argantyr! Now make haste before you become a guest in someone's dungeon!" The three raced off for the outskirts of Aroon-Joon.

---

Tharat sat alone at his supper table savoring the flesh of the slow-roasted urchin who had had the misfortune of becoming lost deep in the woods and ensnared in one of the old wizard's traps. Tharat snapped his teeth as he dipped his spoon into a bowl of boiled potatoes and spooned some more out. No sooner had he brought the oversized wooden spoon up to his mouth than there came a knock at the door. Tharat was immediately wary. No one knew where he lived. It must be someone who had gotten lost and was seeking shelter for the night. A wide grin split the wizard's face and he became excited about the potential opportunity and the possibilities. A slow roasted babe or a small child was tender; but a fully grown adult human would supply him with meat for some time. What if there were more than one person? His heart raced and he snapped his teeth together. The rapping at the door came again.

"One moment!" shouted the wizard as he got up and ran over to the door. "Now, who is it?"

The voice of a young girl answered, "I am just a poor girl with an infant who seeks shelter this night." The excitement was more than Tharat could contain. He hurriedly flung the front door wide and saw a girl standing in the doorway with a bundle. Tharat grinned and gestured for the girl to enter his home as he stammered, "Right this way! Right this way, you poor child. Poor child with a child. How fortunate for me. Fortunate for me, that is, because I am all alone and welcome your company…" His words trailed off as he turned to shut the door to his house, but instead his throat was seized in an iron grip. Argantyr commanded Taren, "Now take your blanket and get back to the horses and wait with your brother. I will join you ere long."

Tharat's eyes were wide with fear as Argantyr held him against the wall and strangled him—recognition upon the dying wizard's face. Argantyr growled at Tharat, "I know you know who I am, Tharat. The witch showed me what Klak and Arju-Lao did to me in her scrying orb. She also showed me your part in it, and for that you are going to pay with your life! Just as they did."

---

Argantyr released Tharat; the wizard had expired some moments agone. Argantyr rummaged through the dead sorcerer's house looking for something of value. Argantyr did not need any gold or jewels; he had taken all that Klak's mercenaries had amassed when he and Thorn had destroyed the Wolf along with his entire army. Argantyr took what spoils he could carry with him, and the rest he had hidden in a secret place to gather upon his return. No, he knew that Tharat dealt in unique magickal objects that the old wizard would trade for the human flesh that he craved.

Argantyr found one room in the house that was locked. He kicked the door in with a loud thud and looked upon the chamber. The room was lined with shelves of books on all sorts of gramarye and dark magicks—books dedicated entirely to subjects as varying as necromancy and shapeshifting to pacts with demons and vampirism. Argantyr's eyes scanned the room by the light of a large candle he had taken from Tharat's dining table; he looked upon daggers and swords of various makes and sizes—most of them covered in runes similar to those that were on Thorn's armor and the dagger that he had used to kill Arju-Lao. He saw scrying orbs, pendulums, and rings and pendants with mystical signs and sigils. With a snort, Argantyr turned to leave the room but stopped as his eyes lighted on a familiar sight. Hanging in the corner was a large wolf's hide like the one Klak had worn and used to shapeshift into the werewolf that had made him nearly invincible in battle. Argantyr stepped forward and took the magickal cloak down from its hanger. He threw it over his shoulder and walked back to the bookshelf. Argantyr removed the book dedicated to shapeshifting titled *On the Black Art of the Fenrir and Becoming the Lycanthrope*. With the book in one hand and the wolf's skin thrown over his shoulder, Argantyr stepped over the dead wizard's body and left the house.

Taren and Tarac had heeded well Argantyr's instructions and waited with the horses. They stared at the weird wolfskin draped over the man's shoulder as they all mounted their horses, but thought it better not to ask any questions of the man who had agreed to be their protector until they reached the more orderly and civilized lands of Arthing.

Argantyr was a man of scant words. After imbibing a few cups of wine around the campfire on the first night of their journey, Tarac asked the warrior, "So what will you do once you reach your native land of Tuatha, Argantyr? Live a life of wine, women and song?" Taren sat listening intently to every word; she was concerned about parting company with this strange man who had saved her virtue and, she was certain, the life of her brother back at the Wolfshead Inn.

Argantyr answered the boy in his deeply resonating voice, "Aye, Tarac, I will live a life of wine, women, and song; but first, I must satisfy my wanderlust. I will go to Gurmania and raise a band of mercenaries; then, carve a kingdom for myself to the north in Scaldavia, perhaps all of the way from Æsirland to Vanirland." Taren and Tarac sat quietly as they realized that they could not follow Argantyr; his life was to be one of conquest, usurped thrones, and blood-soaked crowns. "Best get your blankets and get some sleep," Argantyr told the youths. "There is a long day's ride ahead of us on the morrow."

As Argantyr drifted off to sleep he heard the baying of a lone wolf in the distance; he wondered to himself, *What will it be like...?*

# ...WHERE THERE IS NO SANCTUARY

A man crouched in the snow beneath a dimming sky. Darkness was fast approaching. The man's head was bowed, and he leaned on his broadsword for support. The streaming blood of his enemies covered his naked chest and torso, and blood and foam frothed from his mouth and fell onto the snow-covered earth. His long black beard and hair were spattered with blood. Draped over the man's back was a cape made from the hide of a giant wolf, its head fitting over the man's as a hood. The large scintillating blue jewel in his sword hilt glared a single ray of hope amid the red-stained faces, shorn limbs, and spilled innards of both friend and foe alike. Among the rent corselets, broken swords, and shattered shields of Æsir and Vanir, the cacophony of the recent battle receded in his thrumming eardrums. The man's heart raced, and his lungs labored to drink deeply of the frosty air, while his brain struggled to adjust to his change in perception of his surroundings.

A red-haired warrior appeared and stood over the man crouching in the snow. "At first I thought they were merely tales! A man who led the Æsir, changing to a wolf and killing good Vanir men. Had I not seen it with mine own eyes, I would not have believed the stories about King Argantyr Fenris, the mighty Tuathic warrior who led the Æsir against my people.

"You don't seem so mighty now, Argantyr," the young red-haired man spoke calmly as if within a dream, "I saw you hold my father on the ground. You were ripping his throat open, and blood was *spraying from his neck*!" The young Vanirman's voice changed to a growl as he quickly brought his broadsword down to split Argantyr's head open.

Argantyr brought his sword up and blocked the blow, but the force of the impact sent him rolling onto his back. Argantyr drove his right foot into the man's groin, lifting the Van off of the ground. Before the youth could recover, the Tuathic chieftain was on his feet, knocking his foe's sword out of the way with his own broadsword and quickly coming back with his dagger in his left hand to slit the Van's throat. Blood jetted from the young warrior's neck and reddened the drifts.

While the man was bleeding out on the snow, Argantyr began searching for his armor and a fresh change of furs. He was always prepared for the aftermath of the battle—of his transformation from the werewolf back into a man. He dressed as warmly as possible, hoping to defy the elements just a little longer for he knew not what.

The warrior king reflected on the recent battle: all of the horses were either dead or had run away, and Æbbath, the chaotic flying beast that Argantyr had ridden into battle, had flown off in the melee. Argantyr had been occupied with dispatching a Vanirman to the House of Shades when he had quickly glimpsed the beast rise up from the ground, devouring a man headfirst as it left on leathern wings.

---

His present situation was not good—the snowfall had accelerated into a blizzard. Argantyr turned in what he perceived to be a southerly direction and struggled to walk. He was the last living man in this frozen wasteland, and his animal senses receded now that he had changed back to a man. He didn't have the strength to change to a beast again, having fought on the battlefield in human form, changed to the werewolf and then back to a man. The remainder of the supernatural energy from his beastly transformation was being spent quickly healing the wounds and cuts he had previously sustained on the battlefield as a human, before his change to the werewolf had occurred. *Another transformation into the beast this soon would kill him, but so would the storm if he didn't quickly find shelter in this no man's land of snow and ice.*

Argantyr had staggered only a few steps in the bloody snow drifts when he heard an explosion from behind. It was too loud to be a thunderstorm. *Better to die in an avalanche than to slowly freeze to death.* He spun around, expecting to see a mountain of snow tumbling down on him. Instead, he saw a lofty tower hove into view.

*The structure had not been there ere now.* Argantyr trudged toward the tower, taking in the details as he approached the edifice. The surface of the tower looked to be covered in a massive black serpent's skin with red and yellow mottling. The snakeskin undulated and glistened in the dusk. The top of the tower was so high that he could not see it due to his close proximity and the raging blizzard. The structure was set with large chunks of brightly colored and blazing jewels: sapphires, rubies, emeralds, carnelian, malachite, amber, and others that he had never seen before.

Argantyr scanned the tower for an entranceway. He had to find refuge from the storm now! He could feel his heart beating laboriously and his lungs filling up with ice as he struggled to breathe. He ran his hand over the serpent-skin surface, hoping to discover an entrance, when he heard a thunderous rumbling and the sound of two massive stones grinding together.

A door appeared in the bottom surface of the tower and slowly opened, inviting him to enter. He stumbled through the portal, and the door slammed behind him. He heard the sound of the stones grating together again, and when he looked back over his shoulder, the door through which he had entered the tower was now gone. Where the door had once been, there was only the smooth inside surface of the chamber in which he now stood.

Argantyr's eyes took in the details of the room. The chamber was heated by a single fireplace along the east wall. In the center of the room, there was a large dining table laid out with a spread of food: beef ribs, freshly baked loaves of bread, and vegetables were in abundance, as were grapes, apples and more exotic fruits that were uncharacteristic of the clime.

Argantyr opened the bottle of wine sitting with the food and poured it into the glass beside the plate he found waiting for him. All of this was suspicious, but at the moment his animal instincts were dominant and all he cared about was food, warmth, and shelter from the raging blizzard. He dug into the food and drink with gusto and let the demons howling on the wind outside be damned.

---

"Tell me about her again," the boy pleaded with his uncle.

"Who is this you speak of, Argantyr?" asked old Gromley.

Argantyr's mother, a look of worry on her face, bit her lower lip and shook her head disapprovingly at the boy. Argantyr's father pretended not to notice and looked nervously down at his plate.

Argantyr was too excited to stifle his urge to hear any details that he might have missed before, and he burst out, "Mak Cleigha Clye!"

"Always the same story, boy? There isn't much to tell. Some say your great-grandmother was a witch who disappeared in a snowstorm one night. Some said they seen her runnin' in the direction of the thunder that was rumblin' like the sky was fallin'. Then they didn't see her no more. Nor was there nary trace that she ever was to begin with," Gromley spoke with a mysterious air, slowly moving his outstretched hands apart.

Argantyr's mother got up and quickly started clearing off the dinner table. His father left the room.

Old Gromley lowered his voice, "You know everyone lived in fear of that woman and the evil that she brought down on this land, and they was all glad to be shed of her. You keep asking about her, and she might just come for you, son!"

All of a sudden, Gromley was speaking in a strange language that wasn't meant for human organs to resonate, and his facial features stretched and contorted, covered in scales and mottling after the fashion *of a serpent.*

Argantyr jerked spasmodically and grunted; then, he was awake. It took him a moment to realize that the dream he had just experienced was not real and he was safe, at least for now.

*That dream!* He had had it before.

For a fighting man like Argantyr, the activity of his mind during slumber held little interest for him. He had no memory of any conversation with his parents, or any other family members, regarding an ancestor named Mak Cleigha Clye. He could never recall any kinsmen even mentioning such a tale, but the dream he had just experienced reminded him of the many recurring dreams over the years he had had about this supposed sorceress and great-grandmother of his.

He dismissed Mak Cleigha Clye as a name he only knew from dreams. There were more important questions to be answered at the present, such as where he was at the moment and if there were any immediate threats in the vicinity. There wasn't much he could do now except to explore the tower.

There was enough food left on the table to fill up a sack with provisions for his journey back southward on the morrow. Being a warrior had taught him to always take advantage of opportunities as they presented themselves, for they may not be found again if one hesitated.

Argantyr found a tapestry on the wall of the chamber and tore it down. He laid the cloth out on the floor and began covering it in food, pulling the sides up and tying it. No sooner had he tied up the sack than he heard the rumbling of thunder and the massive stones scraping again. Off to his left another door opened. *Why had he not noticed the portal before?*

Argantyr stepped into an inclining hallway connecting to another chamber and entered the room. The darkened room began lighting up with small, white luminescent entities of various geometrical shapes. The shapes slowly formed into phantasmagorical wisps that resembled human figures. Only seconds had passed before they became ghostly figures inhabiting the room, talking and interacting with one another. He could see their mouths moving, but no sound emitted from the specters. Some of them danced, but Argantyr could hear no music. *It was a dance—a dance of the dead!*

The Tuathic chieftain moved to the center of the room where two of the men stood, appearing to engage in conversation, though Argantyr could hear no sound.

"What goes on here?" he inquired of the men, but they continued their silent conversation, neither seeing nor hearing him. Argantyr gritted his teeth and reached out to grab one of the men by his arm in an effort to get the man's attention, but the warrior king's steel sinews gripped empty air when his clenched fist went through the man's arm.

Out of the corner of his eye, Argantyr caught a glimpse of a woman dressed in scarlet finery. A black silk cloak was draped over her shoulders. The woman's low-cut dress revealed her ample bosom, and the blood-red garment accented her alabaster skin. Her long black wavy hair spilled over her shoulders, and as she came closer, he could see her high cheek bones and darkly painted piercing emerald eyes.

"You are in grave danger…" The woman's mouth was still moving, but he could not hear some of the words. "…come on."

She laid her hand on Argantyr's arm, and he touched her billowing crimson sleeve. Argantyr's eyes widened when his touch did not clutch open air as it had done with the silent, ghostly men.

The inhabitants of the chamber were removing their clothing and filing through a door that the warrior had not previously observed.

"…on." The woman's voice was breaking up, but he could hear part of what she was saying, and she gestured for him to follow the last of the denuded figures from the chamber through the door into the next room. Argantyr did not remove his garments, nor did the strange woman.

"They are pitiful as the dead who walk mindlessly in the underworld, naked and unashamed, as if they just forfeited their earthly possessions and had newly returned to Hel to prepare for their eternal struggle yet again in a new incarnation," Argantyr mused aloud to the woman as they traversed the spiraling hallway that ascended from the previous chamber to the one into which the procession entered. He had no trouble hearing his own voice.

The woman's mouth moved, and her speech partially returned, "…it is! This….it is!" A look of frantic concern spread over her face as she shook her head affirmatively and took ahold of the warrior's hands in the hope that he would understand.

Argantyr and his companion entered the room. The woman gasped and cast a fearful gaze on the southernmost wall of the room, then shifted her vision to the center of the floor in the middle of the chamber. Argantyr's eyes followed the woman's gaze. What he saw was more an inky shadow than anything—like oil spilling onto the floor. Tendrils protruded from the Thing, and Argantyr saw burning eyes ablaze in the center of what he took to be an absence of the Thing's face. Argantyr's hand instinctively reached for his sword hilt, but the woman stayed his hand with her own. The inky shadow's appendages receded into it, and its burning gaze subsided as it shut its eyes.

A curly-headed boy with short horns protruding from his head sat in the middle of the room with his goat-legs crossed. The goat-boy blew into a set of pipes, but Argantyr could hear no sound coming from the musical instrument.

The men and women began fondling and kissing each other. A hazel-haired woman appeared across from the piping young satyr and clutched her large, firm breasts while thrusting her hips in a lewd dance that would have offended even the maenads of the Thiasus Cult in the sunny Cretian Isles. She raised one of her breasts and flicked her tongue across her nipple, her face contorting in ecstasy. Both men and women flocked to the woman at the center of the room and bowed at her feet. A flaxen-haired woman crawled to the dancer and placed her face between the woman's legs. The pale-haired woman's head bobbed as the dancer thrust her groin into the woman's face faster and faster!

Men and women and women and women were coupling on the floor and on randomly placed divans in the room.

The strange woman who had led Argantyr into the room cast an inviting glance upon him and licked her lips. "Take me!" she breathed out heavily. Argantyr could feel the heat radiating from this real, living, flesh-and-blood woman as he pulled her to him and kissed her deeply. She turned around and backed her haunches up into his groin, and he gripped her tiny waist, gently moving her hair out of the way so that he could kiss her all over her neck.

Of a sudden, the hair on Argantyr's nape prickled, and his ever-present wolf senses—though dulled by his human brain—warned him just before the thing happened. He cast his gaze upon the dancing woman who was the centerpiece of the orgy—her eyes went wide with terror as tendrils caressed and wrapped around her creamy, naked flesh—tentacles that entered every orifice and violated her. Her head fell back, and blood gushed from her mouth, splattering onto the floor. Crimson tears flowed from her eyes, and her face turned purple, the veins in her neck bulging from the serpentine appendages that entwined her throat. Blood and organs exploded in silence, scattering in all directions of the room—her mangled torso fell upon the floor. Her carnal worshippers scattered, their naked bodies and faces sprayed with her blood and fluids.

Argantyr whipped his mighty broadsword from its scabbard and was searching the room for the creature. There was no sight of the abomination—only cruel laughter that emanated from each corner of the chamber and bounced maddeningly off the walls in every direction as it travelled the room. The laughter was a mixture of a deep barking sound and a higher-pitched noise like the tearing of fabric.

Two giants clothed only in loincloths made from the hides of jungle cats appeared close to Argantyr and his mysterious companion. The giants carried large scimitars with thick, curved blades. When they walked past Argantyr and the woman, they grinned and nodded their heads, acknowledging the presence of the Tuathic warrior and his companion. The men were at least seven feet in stature, and their massive muscles rippled beneath their oiled skin. Both men's faces were frozen in the same expression with eyes that slanted upward as if pulled back by an unseen hand, wide noses, pointed ears, and a cruel grin. The bald giants had no hair anywhere on their bodies. The two large men rounded up the celebrants of the orgy and herded them toward the south wall of the room. Those who moved slowly were prodded and jabbed with the giants' cruel scimitars. One woman fell on the floor and was bleeding. The procession stepped over the dying woman as if she were invisible and made for the south wall of the room.

Another rumble of thunder and the grating of massive stone upon stone presaged a newly appeared door through which the naked somnambulists exited for another chamber. The diabolic laughter had stopped as abruptly as it had started. The woman led Argantyr behind the procession.

"Let me tell you something! I believe you are the one—the one who can save us all and put an end to *his* reign of terror!" The woman spoke freely to Argantyr once they were in the hallway that linked the chamber they had just been in with the one where the giants were herding the pitiful human cattle.

"Who is *he*?" Argantyr asked.

"Abijeetat! He is a withered old mummy, yet a powerful wizard. He is thousands of years old, but what lives in him came from beyond the stars, and it is far older than man," the strange woman replied.

"Who are those people who march as though they are the dead entering unto Hel?" Argantyr asked.

"They are prisoners of Abijeetat's tower, just as are you and I! Abijeetat is a master of controlling matter through vibration. Some of the people are hundreds, maybe even thousands, of years old, but they are very much alive. Abijeetat preserves them by changing their vibratory rates, and, in turn, changing their physical make-up until he is ready to use them for his amusement. They are then restored to their original forms. By this sorcerous apparatus, Abijeetat's prisoners can live forever, if it is his will. They can feel every cut and blow inflicted upon them! Even in acts of pleasure, they are pushed far beyond their limits, into the agonies of ecstasy!" she said.

"Who are you, woman, and what do you do here?"

"I-I don't know who I am. It has been so long that I have forgotten my name. I remember that I once worked powerful magick, but it was mere child's play compared to the sorcery of Abijeetat! I am a hostess to Abijeetat's 'guests' and I...," she sobbed and looked away from Argantyr, bursting out in tears before continuing. "I lie with the foul mummy and the abomination that lives within him like a whore every night."

"Why are you here?" Argantyr asked, a look of concern appearing on his countenance.

"I came here long ago. I have forgotten the past. It is but a dim shadow in my mind's eye. I know that I summoned the tower in a fit of rage and sorcery. I sought sanctuary from something... where there is no sanctuary. The tower appeared in a snow storm, and I entered it hoping to find the solution to a problem that I have long forgotten. Now, the only problem that I am concerned with is the fact that I am a prisoner of Abijeetat in this tower. We all are! I saw you in a vision! You are the leader of a great band of warriors. There was much slaughter! As Abijeetat's tower spiraled through time, the sorcerer was drawn to the vibrations given off by mass slaughter and death. The pain, the excitement, and the blood lust! These things called to him like a wolf howling in the wastelands of night. Without a doubt he had hoped to find some prisoners. Are you the only survivor?"

"Aye, woman. A small party of wedding guests were returning from King Æthelfrid's daughter's wedding some months agone when they had been set upon by Prince Vaeda's men. Vaeda was the eldest son of the Vanir King, Cnut Bloodaxe. Regarding the fate of Æthelfrid's guests: the men were slaughtered, and the women were defiled. Æthelfrid's youngest son, Rollo, was found with the blood eagle cut into his back. Rollo's lungs were cut out and placed on his back like wings. When Æthelfrid's emissaries confronted the Bloodaxe about it, the Vanir king just roared with laughter and swilled his mead, mocking Æthelfrid. He had arranged the whole affair to provoke Æthelfrid into a war that he had wanted for a long time as a chance to expand Vanir territory and set one of his own sons upon Æthelfrid's throne.

"Æthelfrid has long been my friend, and he asked for my help. I, along with a portion of my royal guard and a small band of Æsir light cavalry, were closing the Haalfgardian borders after defeating Cnut Bloodaxe's army. We thought we had seen the last of them at the Battle of Tarnoth, when what was left of Cnut's army had turned tail and fled, but the Bloodaxe must have rallied every last man left in his kingdom.

"We were ambushed by what was left of them and outnumbered two-to-one. We fought hard today, and no Vanirman lived, but neither did any of my comrades. I personally saw to Cnut Bloodaxe's death, fulfilling my promise to my friend and avenging my fallen sword-brothers. Cnut was like a mad dog who latched on and would not let go... Until he got ahold of a wolf! I tore the Vanir King's throat out and slew the last of his lineage.

"It should be a safe journey back to friendlier Æsir territory on the morrow if this storm subsides, but I had no provisions. I still have no horse, and there is a blizzard going on outside the tower this night. There wasn't much that I could do except to explore the tower."

The woman nodded in agreement.

"What is the purpose of the wizard's tower?" Argantyr asked the woman.

"Some of those who have been here longer than I say the tower itself is a manifestation of Abijeetat's evil and perverse lusts, constructed by his incontestable will. The tower moves through time and many worlds, collecting the doomed for Abijeetat's sadistic revelries, but even Abijeetat has some limitations; it will be dusk before he can move the tower again. The storm will abate the closer we come to daylight. We, all of us, must find a way to escape! You must help us! You are the one!"

"Your voice! It just occurred to me how clearly I can hear it now with no interruptions!" Argantyr said, puzzled.

"All sound is blocked by the Naethelian vibrations that Abijeetat stirs with his Ænokian Calls. Only in his throne room manifests the synchronicity where all beings can connect with no interference. When one reaches that destination it is too late to matter. The Ænokian Calls are a set of tablets numbering nineteen. They are written in a magickal language that was inscribed on the tablets that the Thing which inhabits Abijeetat's body brought down from its world.

"The Thing travelled from far beyond the stars to this world when man was as yet undreamt out of the primal slime that is Ubbo-Sathla. It created its own dimension and lurked there, waiting to be summoned by those who dared. The vibrations follow it as the unnameable shadow slithers from chamber to chamber. Since we are in the hallway, and he is not here, you may now hear my voice. But he knows that you are here! Abijeetat brought you here and he means to have you as the source of his entertainment in the tower tonight!" The woman was speaking more hurriedly, and she looked increasingly fearful.

"I have never met man or wizard who couldn't be bled to death by cold steel, woman!" growled Argantyr.

"You... and... you will tonight!" Her voice wavered in and out, and she took Argantyr by his arm and urgently led him into the chamber where the pitiful horde had been herded only moments agone.

Upon his entrance into the room, Argantyr saw a man tied to a wheel, mounted to a machine that stood upright. The prisoner's arms and legs were stretched out and firmly bound by thick iron shackles. One of the giants quickly spun the man on the wheel. Two more giants, faces fixed in a rictus of hateful joy, threw pointy daggers at the man as the wheel spun. The victim's left eye socket was gorged with crimson, and he bled from the dart-like weapon protruding from his shoulder. His groin was a mass of clotting blood.

Argantyr turned quickly to find the strange woman who had accompanied him had gone. His eyes searched the room for her, but she was not to be found. He spotted a large closed door leading from the chamber. The door was set back in the wall and shadowed by heavy blocks of stone.

Argantyr looked to his left and saw another of the fiendish giants holding a woman while a second giant used a branding iron to burn a hieroglyph into the woman's steaming flesh, her mouth wide open, screaming a silent cry that Argantyr could not hear.

Across from the wall where the giants played their deadly game with the man on the wheel lay a young woman upon a table. Her hands and feet were securely bound with ropes and her impregnated stomach bulged and undulated, rapidly growing. Some of the older women stood around her. The pregnant woman's mouth opened in a silent scream, and her stomach burst open. The inky shadow emerged from her rent torso and sensuously slid its serpentine tendrils over her throat and dead face. The Thing's appendages moved up and gently played with her hair. Argantyr, his face contorted with rage, wrenched his broadsword free of its scabbard and shouted, "Enough!"

None of the human inhabitants occupying the room noticed Argantyr's presence in the chamber, but the Thing that had just burst from the woman's stomach turned its burning gaze upon Argantyr; then, like fading ember, the luminescence of the Thing's deadly stare was gone; and the Thing sank into the woman like oil and vanished.

All around the warrior king, death and madness triumphed as he saw two giants sawing off a man's lower leg at the knee; one of them held their victim while another worked on him with a large curved sword with jagged teeth. Blood jetted from the severed leg as the tortured fellow looked in the direction where Argantyr stood—looked right through him. Argantyr charged in among the giants, leaping high and aiming a blow at the neck of the brute who was removing the man's leg. The grinning expression and upwardly-sloping facial features of the giant never changed, but there was fear in his eyes as his severed head rolled upon the floor. Before the first giant's body could hit the floor, the second brute who had been holding the tortured victim had already drawn his wicked, curved blade and brought it down in an attempt to split Argantyr from head to groin. Argantyr's panther-like reflexes saved him as he moved quickly to one side and brought his own blade back-handed through the giant's knee.

Blood spurted from the brute's wound; he shifted his weight and fell crouching on his uninjured leg. The colossus aimed a horizontal blow intended to spill Argantyr's innards, but the Tuathic chieftain managed to fall back a pace, and his enemy's blade raked his ribs. Argantyr immediately sprang back in and drove his sword into the giant's chest, his full weight behind the thrust. Blood gushed from the brute's mouth and splattered onto the floor of the chamber.

Ere Argantyr could wrench his blade free, one of the giants rushed in and pinioned his arms. The warrior king began uttering the incantations that would free him from his mortal bonds and in turn, free him from the grasp of the brute; but another giant rushed in and struck the warrior with a hard blow across his jaw that nearly snapped his neck, followed by a left hook to the mouth that loosened his teeth. Argantyr saw the giants converge upon him from all corners of the room. They rained blow after blow on him. He was bleeding heavily, and he could feel the pain of broken ribs. His last vision was of the same maniacal expression on all of the faces of the giants. The warrior king's consciousness gave way, and he sank spiraling into darkness.

---

Argantyr's nose and throat stung as he slowly regained his senses. Remnants of the powder that had been blown into his face by one of his assailants to awaken him had settled. His vision slowly returned.

"Kneel before Abijeetat, plaything!" burst a voice from the throne setting upon a raised dais before the warrior.

Argantyr struggled to squint through his swollen face. The voice that commanded him came from a withered mummy sitting on an ornate throne carved from a large chunk of ruby. Jeweled serpents comprised the mummy's headdress. The snakes were bunched close together on the top of his head and fanned out thicker as they ascended, bordered and held in place with gold that had been molded into a frame around them. Upon Abijeetat's chest was a topaz breastplate covered in hieroglyphs and trimmed with bronze. A crimson sash was worn about the lich wizard's waist, and he held a bronze scepter with a thin, sharpened axe blade at the top. The mummy's eyes held the same burning red luminosity that emanated from the inky black Thing's gaze. The wizard's face was drawn up, and his mouth was tight. Time had eroded most of his nose away. Worms crawled from holes in his face, yet he still lived and reigned, raining down terror on all within his tower.

"I kneel before…no one!" Argantyr growled through swollen lips.

The living mummy laughed, a barking cachinnation that echoed through the massive, dimly-lit chamber. "In time you will be no different than the others you saw in the chamber of lusts and the chamber of tortures." The wizard nodded to the mysterious woman who had led

Argantyr through the chambers of his tower; she kneeled silently to the left of Abijeetat's throne with her head bowed. The mummy continued, "You are but a hairless ape brought here for my amusement. But let me briefly entertain you in return for the lifetime of service that you are to provide me before you join the legions of my eternal servants. You *shall* hear of the might and glory of the omnipotent Abijeetat!"

Argantyr fixed his eyes on the lich wizard and listened.

Abijeetat continued, "I was once a slave in what is now long sunken Mung, which has for aeons lain beneath the ocean. I was purchased as a young boy by the senile old wizard Balaam. Because of my precociousness, the old fool required of me to see to the organization and care of his library of scrolls and instruments of gramarye. Due to my usefulness, this placed me at the top of the hierarchy of his slaves, and he had no problem looking the other way when the indulgences in my... *peculiar*... activities and appetites led to another slave's madness or death. Even the peasant girls of the city were available to me; none would question Balaam about an occasional missing wench.

"Balaam was a master of evocation, but he would not dare to fully explore the darkest depths of the gramarye of his demon-worshipping ancestors. He always stood in a circle and called the genii and demons into a triangle, applying the necessary pressure to get them to agree to do his bidding—avoiding calling them into himself at all cost."

"Over time I had become thoroughly familiar with the contents of the old man's scrolls and decided to try some magick of my own. On a night when the twin moons of Jahn were in Dahrtal and Theiis, I laid a drugged peasant girl face down on the altar and entered her from behind while reciting *The Invocation to Thasaidon*, opening the gates to oblivion and letting in the One Who Cannot Be Named. As I climaxed into my receptacle, I slit her throat. It was at that moment that he entered me, and he is still within me even now—stronger than ever! It is for this reason that you will kneel before me and proclaim me your master or die immediately, just as Balaam and countless others who have displeased me have done! *Now!*"

Argantyr, both impressed and appalled by Abijeetat's tale, asked him, "Why is it that you have no regard for life or human dignity, wizard?"

"Because to tread another underfoot like the meaningless insect that he is, to tear a wife from her husband and use and dismember her in front of her partner, or to tear a crying babe from its mother's arms and penetrate it unto death while its mother watches helplessly gives me great pleasure and sends me speeding upon the wings of unbridled ecstasy!"

"Then you must die!" growled Argantyr, raising himself from the floor.

The withered mummy's face stretched with a smirk as Abijeetat nodded his head to the strange woman to whom Argantyr had thought himself befriended. The woman turned and picked up a great broadsword with a large blue jewel set in the hilt and a wolf's head upon the pommel; she handed Argantyr his sword. The lich wizard's eyes widened when, with one panther-like bound, the warrior king came crashing upon Abijeetat's crown with a blow that should have split the mummy's skull wide open.

Argantyr grunted, and the sword rebounded as if he had tried to cut stone with it. Abijeetat roared his barking laughter while the Tuathic chieftain rained down his assault upon the wizard. Argantyr might as well have tried to cut a mountain of steel as to attack the old mummy.

"Stop!" shouted Abijeetat as a fiery blast shot from his upraised palm and knocked Argantyr onto the floor, his sword flying out of his hand.

"You needed to see a minor demonstration as to why all who enter this tower become subject to my every whim, or die. It is that simple. It is common knowledge among those versed in the black arts writ down by the greatest devil worshippers of antiquity that he who houses the One Who Cannot Be Named may die by the hand of no mortal man; nor can he be harmed by any weapon wielded by your pathetic kind."

"That is all that I needed to know," Argantyr whispered to the wizard, grinning as he said the words and pulled the wolf-headed hood of his cloak over his head.

"Freae Nome gonastre! Kreedolph hgnome Fenrir! Krynestrees Ryedorf! Hoathehe Fenrir!" Argantyr spat through his swollen mouth and bloody teeth.

Abijeetat leaned forward on his ruby throne, and his eyes widened as his sable, forked tongue flickered from his mouth.

The change came on quickly—Argantyr's face transfigured into an elongated snout, and his eyes burned with hellish, bestial fury. His body, now covered in silver hair, stretched and grew to enormous girth and stature. The hair bristled on the back of the werewolf as he growled and lunged at the unclean abomination sitting upon its throne. Abijeetat raised and extended his palm to blast the werewolf with a fiery shot as he had done to the battered human warrior who had lain before him only a moment ere now, but he had not been as quick as the giant supernatural wolf bearing down on him. The werewolf leaped, driving Abijeetat's upraised hand back and pinning the mummy to his throne.

The giant wolf ripped the wizard's throat out while Abijeetat's mouth gaped wide, cracking long-withered jaws; the lich's eyes widened as the beast's penetrating gaze mirrored the eldritch burning coals set back in the mummy's head. The werewolf's mouth tore off Abijeetat's arms and legs and dust flew from the mummy while the beast ripped the lich wizard to shreds. The werewolf latched its powerful jaws onto Abijeetat's head, and the wizard's head cracked like a nut, his brains oozing out onto the floor.

A scream issued forth from the rent torso of the lich wizard as an inky shape burst forth from what was left of its chest and glided across the floor. The werewolf pounced on the thing, pinning it to the floor, and sinking his teeth into it. The Thing screeched—a high-pitched, terrible sound that was its own death knell—just before bursting into flames. The werewolf held the Thing in its mouth momentarily as it burned, making sure the fire was consuming it; then, the beast flung the Thing to a corner of the throne room where it lay upon the floor, a small pool of burning oil, rapidly consumed by fire.

---

Argantyr knelt on all fours, breathing deeply as foam dripped from his mouth onto the floor of the recently deceased wizard's throne room. The strange woman who had befriended him since his stay in the tower was helping him to his feet while his perception of the surroundings in which he found himself returned to him—the beast receded into his brain, waiting to be called again when needed.

The woman had found Argantyr's clothing and provisions from the chamber where he had left them, and she hurriedly assisted him with getting into his furs and armor, all the while looking nervously about. Thunder rumbled and the tower began to vibrate as if to confirm the necessity of the woman's haste.

"We must be away now!" the woman said excitedly.

"Now?" Argantyr asked like a child waked up in the middle of the night.

The tower rumbled and shook.

"We must escape the tower now, or die!" the woman screamed over the clamor of the rumbling structure.

Argantyr could hear the faint noise of stone grating upon stone as he saw a portal open in the southern wall of the dead wizard's throne room.

"To me, woman!" Argantyr shouted, his warrior's senses returned to him by the threat of imminent danger.

The woman took his hand, and they fled through the door leading out of the tower. By Argantyr's calculations, they would have to make a leap from the tower, but they exited the rumbling structure on solid ground.

"Run! We must get as far from the tower as possible!" the woman cried.

The two of them ran as fast as they could for some time. Argantyr stopped to look back and saw the tower crumbling and exploding into dust that circulated and was dissipating in the northern winds. The woman wasn't far behind him, but she had stopped and was gasping for air. Argantyr walked a few paces back towards her. The woman motioned with her hand for Argantyr to stay put. She hesitated momentarily, then began walking towards him

"I remember my name," she said.

"What is this?" Argantyr asked, his brain only slowly processing what the woman had said.

"I know who I am now!" the woman shouted—the look of confusion on her face changing to horror and madness.

"I am Mak Cleigha Clye!"

Argantyr stood staring at the woman while she extended her right arm in his direction and strode forth. A cry escaped the woman, one that sounded like she was screaming and having her throat cut at the same time—she began to crumble to dust as she walked. The decomposed debris that had been Mak Cleigha Clye blew in the northern wind and mingled with what little had remained of the dust of Abijeetat's tower and its prisoners who had now been freed in death.

The warrior king gazed for some time in the direction where both woman and tower had recently stood.

"It is as if they never existed," Argantyr said aloud. But he knew better, by the aching in his cracked jaw, his painful broken ribs, and the presence of the sack of food taken from the lich wizard's table. The healing effects of changing to wolf and back to man were quickly taking place, and he could feel his loose teeth tightening up in his gums and his ribs, battered organs, and limbs mending.

Argantyr had been walking only minutes in the frozen wasteland when he spotted a tiny dot high in the sky. He quickly unsheathed his broadsword and waved it above his head, crying, "Ho, Æbbath! Ho! I am here!"

The black dot dropped in the sky until the warrior king could see the flying beast clearly. Speeding downward, the creature came to light on a snow-covered embankment close to Argantyr. Æbbath was blood-red in color and had the appearance of a giant, winged salamander with a mouth full of teeth resembling deadly stalactites and stalagmites. Argantyr slung the sack of provisions that he had taken from the wizard's tower onto the creature's back and secured it. The warrior leaped upon the beast's back and took hold of the harness. A clicking sound came from Argantyr's mouth, and he spurred Æbbath's sides with his booted heels. Creature and rider were born aloft on Æbbath's leathern wings. They had plenty of time to make it to the nearest Æsir outpost before dark if they stayed their southerly course at a steady velocity.

# THANNHAUSEFEER'S GUEST

The wine-dark sea swallowed the remains of the scattered wreck and retched up a lone figure too strong to die just yet. Breakers rolled in under the grey sunless sky and cast the man face down on the snowy shore. All about him lay bleached human skulls and assorted bones scattered alongside desolate rocks and boulders.

The man's long black hair stuck to his bearded face. He wore a water-logged cape of giant silver wolf skin and drenched accoutrements fashioned from various other animal hides. His sword still rested in the scabbard slung over his back, and a dirk hung in its sheath at his hip. Echoes of the splintering ship and the screams of dying men staining the deck red with blood rang in his thrumming eardrums.

The man gasped for air—his chest rattling—breathing in the stinging salt air and spitting up acrid brine. He slowly raised himself on all fours and struggled to get to his feet. Drops of bright crimson pattered down onto the back of his left hand and the floor of the barren shore. He touched his moist warm forehead and looked at his hand. From the looks of the blood and the throbbing in his skull he had suffered a powerful blow to the head.

His vision was blurry, and he staggered and fell—tried to raise himself up again. He caught a flash out of the corner of his eye of a billowing white gown blowing in the wind. The woman leaned down, and he wrapped his arm around her. She braced him and helped him to his feet.

Rolling his head to one side, he glanced at her, his vision wavering in and out. Flaxen hair framed her pale-skinned classic beauty with high cheek bones and full red lips that seemed to have never smiled. Her icy blue eyes looked through him upon dim netherworld vistas far beyond the realm of man. She appeared familiar, but he didn't know who she was. They had walked for only a moment when she languorously raised her right arm and pointed to the colossal citadel at the top of the hill in the distance.

"You must go there," she said in the monotone of a black lotus dreamer. He nodded his head and did not argue. He knew he was bleeding from a head wound and winter had set in. It was best that he find shelter and a warm place to dry.

*A massive splash just to the rear of the ship and walls of sea rose up and washed over the deck, drowning some crewmen and throwing others* overboard. A crash like lightning followed by a thunderous roll. The galley's bow shot up and twisted, and the ship exploded from bow to stern. Planks flew high into the air. The main mast collapsed, and the lines dangled high above the galley like striking serpents.

*I was hanging onto the gunwale–shouting*, he recalled. *Where was I going?*

Helped along by this single strange woman with her white gown blowing in the wind, the lone survivor of the shipwreck faded in and out of consciousness. Somehow, he traversed the distance from the shore and was nearing the titanic edifice at the top of the hill.

*Trebuchet! One shot hits us and we're sinking!* he remembered shouting and clenching the gunwale.

*The ship exploded. Men screamed as the mast crashed to the deck and crushed them. The tattered sail whipped in the wind. The deck ran red with the blood of the men who weren't immediately cast into the sea.*

*Yet I live. Here I am, but where am I?*

Lying at the top of the steps and leaning on his arm, the shipwreck survivor pounded his fist on the door that climbed high into the sky. His head fell to one side, and he rolled onto his back and mustered all of his strength to knock yet again on the towering door to the castle. The woman in white was nowhere to be seen. A loud slamming—and the door creaked open as the injured man's head fell back. He slid into black oblivion as if it were a hot bath on a cold winter night.

---

"You took quite a blow to the head and lost some blood, but the cut wasn't as deep as we thought," a woman's voice said.

The man's hand shot out and gripped her by the wrist.

"It's all right," she whispered. "I just need to replace the poultice on your forehead. The salve has done wonders for you in these last two days."

"Two… Two days?" The man mumbled, becoming aware of his surroundings, his blurred vision gradually clearing.

"My sword?! My cloak?!" he exclaimed.

"Your sword is in its scabbard in the corner, and your cloak and clothes are hanging over by the fire. They are surely dry by now."

The fire crackled and gave off a pleasant aroma of well-seasoned cedar.

"Are you cold? I will get you another blanket."

"No," he mumbled, reaching for her. "Shipwreck. Trebuchet fired… Trebuchet fired on us."

She smiled down at him as though he was a child. "There was a shipwreck, but I don't know anything about a trebuchet. I think you are still getting over the fever dreams. You were restless most of last night. So, you came from the wrecked ship? Were there any other survivors?"

The man looked off into the distance, trying to peer back through the misty veils of time and recollect the events of recent days. "No. Only I survived the attack."

The woman's bell-like laughter rang throughout his sleeping chambers. "Maybe the gods of the sea attacked you. There was a terrible storm on the evening you showed up at my lord's castle. My name is Lydiana." She gently brushed his chest with her hand.

He could now see her clearly. Flaming red hair that rippled like waves in the sea fell to her waist. She had piercing blue eyes set back in a handsome face, and her bright blue velvet gown hugged her voluptuous feminine form.

The man's brows furrowed as if he was trying to find a solution to an immediate problem.

"What is your name, man from the sea?" she asked in a childlike voice.

"I... I don't know."

"Well, how about I call you Manannan? You look to be a Tuath, and it is said that Manannan mac Lir is the sea god of the Tuath je Danaan."

The man remained silently pensive.

Her tinkling peal rang throughout the room again, and she said, "Manannan it is!" and turned and left the room.

*A boulder splashed behind the galley far to the rear—then another. He was gripping the gunwale shouting, "Boulders! They are shooting boulders at us!" The third one connected! The ship exploded into splinters from bow to stern.*

The smell of food nearby reminded him he hadn't eaten in a long time. His attention returned to the room, in which he lay, with a crackling fire and a beautiful woman tending to him. Lydiana had returned carrying a tray loaded with roasted boar, boiled potatoes, and a freshly baked loaf of soft warm bread. She set the tray on a nightstand by the bed and went over to a shelf and removed a bottle.

"A vintage red wine. Forty years old," she said as she crossed the room, uncorking the bottle.

"A big strong warrior like you doesn't need a cup. Just take the bottle and drink it. I bet you are used to taking whatever you want." She licked her lips and cast a wanton glance at him.

"Once you have eaten and rested a little more, I will give you a bath; and we can see if I'm right.

"Tomorrow you will meet the lord of the realm, Thanhausefeer. He is hosting a competition. Warriors from all over come to pit steel against steel. The last man standing will be generously rewarded by my lord with all of the gold and jewels the champion can carry away in his ship."

"I saw no ships on the shore, woman."

"They only arrived yesterday. Thanhausefeer wants to meet you on the morrow. He is a great admirer of warriors such as yourself, and I am sure he will want to see you compete in his games."

"And if I refuse to fight?"

Silence filled up the room like the belly of python that had just swallowed its prey. The crackle of the fire even seemed to get quieter as if it were sentient and wished to hide. Lydiana fixed her burning blue gaze on him. "Manannan, my lord is a generous man; but his anger is terrible."

Her eyes softened, and she went over to him and gently ran her hands across his chest and torso and down to his groin. "But let's not worry about that right now. Let's get you cleaned up and nice and relaxed for tomorrow." She smiled at him—a smile he did not return.

---

Manannan marveled at the colossal archways, doors, and vaulted ceiling as Lydiana led him down the corridor to the great hall where the Lord of the Realm held court. The roof was supported by columns that raised the ceiling high into the sky—at least twice the height of any castle he had visited until now. The hall was abnormally wide, and he guessed that the walls were nearly twenty feet thick. Torches the length of spears blazed in sconces high up the walls beyond his reach. He could hear the clash of weapons down the hall.

"What strange architecture," he commented.

Lydiana's eyes narrowed, and she smiled as if enjoying a private jest. They hadn't gone far when she veered off to the left into the monumental archway opening into the great hall.

Two men were engaged in conflict—broadsword against battle-axe—and droplets of blood and sweat were flying; but that did not interest Manannan so much as what sat in the center of the table stripping meat from a human femur. The man was at least twice Manannan's height of six feet, and his massive girth filled out the Giant's scintillating golden throne that was wider than Manannan was tall. Men—some of them armed and armored—sat in long-legged chairs to either side of the Giant observing the games. They looked like dolls on a shelf sitting alongside the behemoth. The Giant, engrossed in watching the two men hack each other to death, paid no heed to Manannan and Lydiana.

"Thannhausefeer?" Manannan asked her.

"Indeed!" Lydiana replied. Her azure eyes beamed, and she grinned—her cheeks like apples.

The Giant's red, square-cut mane was a shock of tangled hair held back by a massive leather band encircling his head. The head band held a large polished oval of azurite centered in front. Cold blue eyes bore into the two warriors endeavoring to deal death to each other. Thannhausefeer's crimson beard fell down his chest and was braided at the ends by ornaments fashioned from the stringed bones of human fingers. Enormous steel sinews rippled under the deceptive roll of fat that partially concealed them. He was dressed in a silver-studded black tunic that fell below his waist and white wool britches. His boots were made of stitched animal hides and were as big as panniers. Red spiked leather gauntlets covered his forearms. He wore no crown; he needed none to proclaim himself the master of his demesne.

Thannhausefeer's golden throne was embedded with rough-cut jewels. Sapphires, rubies, amethysts, and numerous others glinted in the dim sunless light that filtered through the window high above in the dingy hall. The Giant carried no weapons on his person, but a broadsword the length of two horses hung on the wall behind his gleaming throne. Logs crackled and popped in the tall fireplace on the south wall of the chamber, vanquishing the winter chill.

A young bearded blond warrior wielding a broadsword bled from myriad wounds and gasped for breath. His axe-wielding opponent's visage was obscured by a silver-studded executioner's hood made of black leather. The hooded figure was splattered with blood, but most of it wasn't his own. The armor the swordsman had entered the contest in was of inferior quality to that worn by the axe-wielder and had been mostly hacked away by now.

"At him, Kurlick! The fight isn't over until one of you falls!" Thannhausefeer's voice rolled like thunder and reverberated through his chamber as he continued to gnaw the remaining meat from the femur.

At the Giant's command, the yellow-haired warrior hastily looked for an opening and took it. With all of his remaining strength, he moved in with a disemboweling thrust. His opponent had anticipated his next move and side-stepped the man's broadsword just in time. Twisting and coming back through with his battle-axe, the Executioner severed the man's head from his body with one blow. The head spun through the air and landed on the table in front of Thannhausefeer.

"Yes! That's it!" The Giant's laughter rumbled throughout the hall, shaking the feasting table as he pounded his fists on it. Thannhausefeer fervorously smeared droplets of blood on his face from the decapitated head. He reached into a large copper cauldron setting on the table next to him and threw gold coins at the feet of the axe-wielding Executioner.

"Congratulations, Donthar! Three victories yesterday and two so far

## THE SNAKE-MAN'S BANE

today. You may yet live to sail away in your ship with enough wealth to buy your own kingdom!"

The Giant pounded his fist on the dining table again and shouted, "Arrival!"

Four raven-haired beauties in brightly colored gowns appeared from the corridor to the right of Thannhausefeer's throne and started to carry away Kurlick's head and body.

"I marked the page for that one in my book. I knew he would fall next. See that the meat is prepared strictly by the guidelines that I have set forth, or you know what will happen."

The women hurried away.

Thannhausefeer turned and acknowledged Manannan and Lydiana for the first time since they had entered his chamber. "Ah! A new warrior enters the game! You are just in time for the chance of a lifetime. What is your name, Champion?"

The man stood studying Thannhausefeer in silence for a moment. He noticed the Giant begin to fidget and become irritable, but it did not faze him.

"I am Manannan," the warrior said after a long pause.

"Where are you from, Manannan, and how did you hear of my games?"

"I came from the sea."

"The sea?"

"The ship I was sailing in was wrecked. Everyone drowned but me. I know nothing of your games but what I just saw."

"Well, no matter, Manannan from the sea. Sit with us awhile and observe. I am sure you will find what we do to your liking if you have yourself ever shed blood for a living, and by the look of that sword you carry and the scars on your face, I am certain that you have.

"Bring mead and a plate for our new guest!" Thannhausefeer called over his shoulder.

Manannan relaxed his hand on his dagger hilt. "I don't eat the flesh of my own kind, Giant."

"Neither do these men who sit with me, Man from the Sea." Thannhausefeer's face reddened, but otherwise he showed no emotion. The Giant spoke with obvious restraint; his voice dropped lower, and he added, "Be careful not to fall in battle in this hall."

---

The two champions squared off, warily circling each other in the middle of Thannhausefeer's chamber. One was bald, save for the horse tail of hair done in the manner of a circus mare sprouting from the top of his head.

His name was Tarkatha the Bull. Clad in only a loincloth and low boots of animal hide, he brandished a wicked curved scimitar in his fist. His yellow skin glistened with oil. Tarkatha snarled, and his nostrils flared around the large golden ring set in his nose.

The other man was Prince Pellipedes of the Sathzarian Isles. He had gone in secret to Thannhausefeer's castle. Though the Prince was learned in the arts of war, Pellipedes's father, King Diodedes, forbade him to ride into battle. Pellipedes didn't care about a ship-load of treasure: he only wished to impress his father. The Prince, well trained in the double-sword art of A'Tom, wielded a blade with each hand. He was dressed in mailed hauberk, colorful silken finery, and a green silk band, which encircled his head. Every lock of light-brown curly hair was in place, and he had a thin mustache; but by the whirling sword dervish he presented to his opponent, all present could tell the Prince was no mere dandy.

Tarkatha feinted, and Pellipedes jumped back slightly, though his expression remained calm and his blades kept whirling. Pellipedes's blade licked out like a striking serpent, and rivulets of blood fell from Tarkatha's upper arm. The Bull seemed not to notice and answered with a slash aimed at Pellipedes's midsection. The Prince jumped back again. Tarkatha closed in and slashed. This time the point of his scimitar connected with Pellipedes's abdomen and tore through mail, raking the Prince's skin.

Pellipedes came in, twin swords spinning; and Tarkatha artfully dodged having his arms shorn from each side of his body. The Bull looked as though he was performing a dance to avoid the Prince's flurry of steel. Tarkatha aimed another disemboweling thrust, and the Prince backed up to avoid having his innards spilled on the floor.

Manannan was so engulfed in the combat taking place before him that he didn't notice himself and Thannhausefeer as they sat side by side, swilling mead and slamming their drinking jacks down in unison as though it were choreographed.

Tarkatha blocked Prince Pellipedes's left-hand blade with his scimitar and slammed a booted foot into Pellipedes's face when the Prince went for too wide of a stroke with his right-hand sword. The Prince stumbled, trying to regain his balance, and fell. As Pellipedes leapt to his feet, Tarkatha moved in and slit the man's throat with the point of his scimitar. The Prince fell back to the floor gurgling as the blood jetted from his jugular.

"Outstanding!" Thannhausefeer boomed. "Here we see age and experience has just vanquished extreme martial skill until now untried in the face of death!"

"Arrival!" the Giant bellowed, and the four dark-haired beauties appeared again. "This one is to be prepared for his funeral, but I don't think that is what Tarkatha has in mind."

## THE SNAKE-MAN'S BANE

Thannhausefeer addressed Tarkatha the Bull, "You have done well, warrior; and I keep my promise to you. You shall have Pellipedes's body to do with as you like while you bed the one of your choice tonight."

Tarkatha looked at the four women who had come to carry away the corpse, and with a quick snapping motion of his arm thrust his index finger at one of the young women. She couldn't have been more than sixteen years old. The girl began to tremble.

"You will go with Tarkatha and Pellipedes's corpse tonight, Rose-Athelind!" the Giant croaked like an enormous bullfrog.

The girl fled back through the corridor weeping.

"Remember: there is nowhere you can run to escape my will, woman!" Thannhausefeer's laughter reverberated through the chamber. He turned his head, looking back through the archway where the girl had just run. "I make good my promise to Tarkatha this night!"

Manannan quaffed deeply of his cup and sat back relaxed in his chair to the right of Thannhausefeer. A gong sounded at the back of the chamber, and a man appeared in a black studded tunic much like the one Thannhausefeer wore. The man's closely-cropped black hair set above a low forehead that had sustained a number of sword gashes. His face was smeared with dark-blue and green paint of woad that did little to conceal the scars deeply etched into his countenance like a roadmap to Hel. The warrior wore leggings of animal hide and a scabbarded sword and dirk. He stood at attention in front of Thannhausefeer and his table of warriors—all, Manannan had surmised, there to compete for the shipload of wealth the Giant had promised the winner.

"Care to cross swords with General Krothess, Manannan from the sea? I think I need to see some proof of your martial skills before we go much further. The way you are swilling my mead supply, I soon shall have none left if I do not find a diversion for you."

The warriors sitting at the table laughed in unison at the Giant's jest.

Manannan drained his cup and squinted his eyes at the General, smiling lopsidedly. He slowly got up from his chair beside Thannhausefeer and walked around the table to meet General Krothess.

The wind whistled off Manannan's blade as he whipped his sword from its scabbard. General Krothess drew his sword and stepped into a fighting stance. Krothess made the first move with a blow aimed at Manannan's head. Manannan ducked the general's blade and drove Krothess back and back, raining blow after blow upon the General's sword. Krothess threw up his blade just in time to keep Manannan's blade from splitting his skull. Momentarily the two warriors stood pressing steel on steel. The stench of the General was overpowering. He smelled like an amalgamation of sour clothes, dung, and rotten wood.

*The boy stunk of sour clothes and was a whole head taller than him, but he still gave a good account of himself. He had suffered the big boy's taunts and torment for far too long.*

*He heard his mother calling his name to come to supper as he hit the bully with a stick he had hidden in the woods in anticipation of the fight with him that afternoon. The big boy lay on the ground, unconscious and bleeding. From then on, he never saw him in the woods surrounding his house again.*

*I just heard my mother calling my real name, but I was so busy fighting that I didn't hear what it was*, realized Manannan.

Manannan braced himself and shoved the General backwards. Before Krothess could regain his bearings, Manannan slashed through Krothess's hands where they gripped the handle of the man's sword. The General's left hand was ruined, and he shifted his sword so that he only wielded it right-handed. With a stout blow, Manannan knocked Krothess's sword back so that the man was unprotected and cleft the General from collarbone to sternum on the return. General Krothess fell to his knees, blood frothing from his mouth, then headed over.

Manannan cleaned his blade on Krothess's clothes, and returned it to his scabbard. "You might want to wash that one well before you eat him, Giant. He stunk pretty bad."

Thanhausefeer sat in silence, his eyes shifting back and forth from Manannan to Krothess's corpse on the floor of his great hall.

"Arrival!" the Giant boomed.

---

*Lydiana lay asleep next to Manannan. After the two of them had sated their lusts she quickly dozed off. Manannan was spent, but his mind raced back through time trying to force open doors to the past for the answers he needed.*

*Lydiana had offered herself, nay, forced herself upon him. As he had taken her from behind, he looked down at her. When she turned her head to look back at him, it wasn't Lydiana but the Woman in White who had brought him from the shipwreck to Thannhausefeer's castle. The woman gritted her teeth; covering her entire back was a tattoo of a large wolf. His eyes moved from the wolf to her perfect pale visage; her ruby lips smiling up at him.*

*"To show you I will always remember you…" she moaned.*

Mannanan jerked awake and sat up in bed. Lydiana mumbled something and rolled over only to fall back asleep.

*I am not Manannan! She just said my name. But who am I?*

The harder he tried to come away with what he needed to know about himself, the more the woman's voice receded into fast-fading dream. The tattoo of the wolf spread out across the woman's back was the last thing he remembered as he slipped yet again through the gates of slumber and behind the wall of sleep.

---

*Steel on steel clashed! Horses' whinnies and neighs blended with the screams of men. Battle-axes shattered helmets, and fine-pointed blades pierced corselets and spilled vital organs upon the ground. Maces crashed into skulls, and brains seeped out onto the frozen earth. Every minute, men died in scores. The tide of battle had turned against them. Realizing this, he threw his head back and shouted to the sky. The pain was at first excruciating, however brief, then he fell to his knees and his perception changed. His senses were heightened to ecstasy, and everything around him moved in slow motion.*

"Wake up, Manannan!" Lydiana shook him.

"What did I just say?" He was trying to remember the words he had called out in the throes of nightmare.

"I don't know. You were speaking some sort of gibberish. It sounded like a chant. You aren't a sorcerer are you, Man from the Sea?" Lydiana pounced on him playfully, revealing her ample alabaster cleavage. She licked his lips, sticking her tongue in his mouth.

"Today is the final day of the games. Thannhausefeer will want to get an early start. And if you are lucky, you will sail away with a shipload of treasure at dawn on the morrow."

"And if I am unlucky, woman?"

Lydiana looked down and cast her glance away from Manannan.

"Will you come away from this island with me, Lydiana?"

"It cannot be," she sighed.

"Why?"

"My place is here, tending to Thannhausefeer's affairs and warming his bed. He does you honor by allowing you to sleep with me."

"This man is a monster! A cannibal! Why do you stay with him?"

She looked away from Manannan as she spoke. "My mother was cast up from the sea in a shipwreck, just like yourself. She died giving birth to me. She was all too human…"

"And your father?"

Lydiana—nostrils flaring—turned her piercing blue eyes on Manannan.

"Thannhausefeer!"

Knives formed a whirling silver ring before Thannhausefeer and the three warriors sitting at the Giant's table. Dwarfs with twisted limbs clad in colorful dyed sleeveless wool tunics sat behind Thannhausefeer's throne playing a gay tune on flutes made of human bones and drums fashioned from skulls stretched with human hide. Lydiana entered through the door at the back of the chamber and came over to sit in the empty chair to Manannan's right.

"He is good, isn't he, lover?" she spoke into Manannan's ear and nodded at the fool dressed in bright red and green silk tights covered in diamond-shaped patterns. The man's face was calm and stoic under the tall conical-shaped hat he wore. Standing across from the Giant, the dagger-whirling juggler looked like an obnoxious toy that a hateful child derives great pleasure from slowly destroying.

"That's enough, Jobenox! It is time to fight again!" Thannhausefeer rumbled.

The fool kept the daggers whirling as he turned to go and exited through the main archway of the great hall, his face set as stone.

"You were late to Thannhausefeer's table. What you did not hear is those daggers are all dipped in poison. The merest scratch—and the fool dies. He puts himself into a trance when he performs." Lydiana raised her eyebrows but elicited no response from Manannan other than a grunt.

"Well, well. There are three of you left: Donthar the Executioner, Tarkatha the Bull, and Manannan, the Man from the Sea. I think it is high time we see who gets to carry away a shipload of treasure at dawn tomorrow," the Giant bellowed.

The gong sounded and Thannhausefeer's voice boomed again, "Tarkatha and Manannan!"

The two warriors walked around the table, and broadsword and scimitar hissed from their scabbards like metallic serpents. Both men stepped into fighting stances: Manannan, holding his heavy broadsword two-handed, and Tarkatha the Bull, holding his wicked curved blade in his right hand. Tarkatha was the first to strike, feinting, then aiming a blow at Manannan's inner thigh. Manannan brought his broadsword around and blocked Tarkatha's blade, nearly sending it spinning from the Bull's grip. Tarkatha leapt back and grasped his scimitar with both hands. Thannhausefeer roared with laughter at the man's overconfidence. Sweat beaded Tarkatha's forehead, rolling down into his slanted black eyes.

Broadsword and scimitar engaged in a quick succession of lightning-fast strokes. Manannan's sword missed splitting Tarkatha's head by a fraction of an inch, and Tarkatha answered with a blow that would have severed Manannan's arm had he not stepped back. Even so, Tarkatha's blade sliced through Manannan's shirt and broke the skin.

Tarkatha brought his blade down and over. Manannan stepped aside, and Tarkatha's sword hissed another blow on the return. Manannan blocked the blow and made an arc with his broadsword. Manannan's steel bit into Tarkatha's hamstring, but as the Bull went down on one leg, he brought his sword back through at Manannan's lower torso. Manannan knocked the scimitar from Tarkatha's grip and struck the man's head from his shoulders with a single wide sword stroke.

Manannan held the yellow man's head up, and showed it to Thannhausefeer, then dropped it on the floor.

"Say 'hello' to Pellipedes in Hel, Tarkatha!" Manannan mumbled.

Thanhausefeer's fat belly rolled with laughter, and he clapped his hands. Only three of the serving girls appeared this time to take away Tarkatha's corpse and mop the combat area. Manannan noticed that Lydiana had left the room. He went over to sit by the Giant and quaff deeply of his mead cup.

*Thannhausefeer was nothing more than a tyrannical oversized cannibal, but—by Fenris!—his mead was good; and killing was thirsty work!*

Manannan's hand instinctively brushed the giant silver wolf's pelt thrown over his back like a cape while half-emptying his cup with one pull.

"Best go easy on your cups, Man from the Sea. You fight Donthar the Executioner next, and he is not so happy with you. Ever since he showed up, he has been wanting to bed Lydiana; but I gave her to you. Now, she is going to show him something to send the fire coursing through his veins." Thannhausefeer nodded his head as the flame-haired beauty appeared before the Giant's table.

Lydiana grinned and her lust-filled eyes met with those of the Giant as they shared more than just a private jest. The dwarfs introduced the tune with a drum beat that reached into the primal area of the brain governing the procreative drive, and the flutes joined in with an eerie minor-key melody. The music bespoke the dangerous seduction of beauty, and Lydiana began slowly and sinuously undulating her hips. She cupped her hands to the slender silver brassiere barely covering her firm breasts and spun in a circle billowing her green gossamer skirt.

All three men, including Thannhausefeer, watched, enspelled. Lydiana thrust her hips, and the drums became more aggressive; and the music louder. She ripped the fabric from her lower body and sensuously stepped out of it like a serpent shedding its skin. Manannan's cup stopped before it could reach his lips as he sat motionless staring at what was beneath the skirt: another skirt of coarse material with the drawing of a wolf inked upon it. He had seen it before. It was the tattoo on the woman's back; the woman from his dreams.

He suddenly recalled the woman from his dream say, "To show you I will always remember you… Argantyr!"

*Argantyr? That is my name! Argantyr—Argantyr Faoladh as I am known in my homeland of the Tuath je Danaan! And King Argantyr Fenris in the northlands of Skaldavia where I rule!*

Lydiana thrust her hips faster and faster, and the wolf's head jerked and thrust at Manannan-Argantyr, faster and faster! Memories rushed forth and retreated like lightning bolts flashing across the sky and vanishing. Lydiana removed her scant silver scaled top, and her firm bare breasts jiggled.

Even over the music Argantyr could hear the sound of Thannhausefeer swallowing as the giant leaned over and told him, "How do you like her skirt? A gift to my daughter! I have to commend the tattoo artist who put that wolf on the girl's back. He was exceptional! I traded for the woman taken in a raid, but there was an obedience problem that took great measures to correct. Oh! She screamed and screamed but was defiant to the end! Donthar there is normally excellent at getting someone to do what he wants. He removed her skin while she yet lived, when he was here about a month ago."

"The trebuchet! One shot and he's sinking us!" he had shouted as he clenched the gunwale.

*I can see through the mists on that fog-bound hill! I can see what was on that hill as clear as day now! There was no trebuchet! It was him! The Giant was standing on the hill throwing boulders at us! He knew King Friodere had sent us to rescue his daughter, Friona! My love! Friona! I was too late to save you, but I am not too late to avenge your death!*

Argantyr saw the looks exchanged between Thannhausefeer and Lydiana.

*The Giant knows I have come here to kill him. With the luck of the Tuath, he still thinks that I don't know who I am. Best to let him keep thinking that until I am ready.*

Argantyr's eyes met Lydiana's, and he arched his eyebrows and smiled, drinking deeply of his cup. With a gesture from his hand, Thannhausefeer signaled for the dance to stop. The music was cut short, and Lydiana suddenly ceased her wicked gyrations. With a gesture from Thannhausefeer's hand, Lydiana turned and left the room. The gong sounded. No further words were needed. Argantyr and Donthar met in front of Thannhausefeer's table.

Whoosh! Donthar's axe went at Argantyr, and he ducked the deadly blade. Again and again Donthar the Executioner came on, and his axe blade bit empty air, coming ever closer with each swing. Of a sudden, Argantyr lunged forward; and splinters flew from the Executioner's axe as Argantyr's blade hacked into the handle. Blood ran in rivulets from Donthar's fingers down the handle of his battle-axe. He switched his grip on the weapon, and when he did, Argantyr's broadsword ripped through Donthar's hauberk and made a shallow gash in his chest as the Executioner leaned back.

The two men slashed at one another like rabid dogs. Argantyr bled from gashes in his chest and upper arms, and Donthar's hauberk was shredded. The Executioner's blue tunic was soaked with his own blood as he bled from what would have been several fatal sword strokes aimed at a slower, lesser warrior.

Donthar brought his axe over and down in a stroke to split Argantyr's head open had it not been for the man's panther-like reflexes. Donthar slammed the haft of his axe into Argantyr's ribs with a blow that would have knocked most men to the ground. Argantyr kicked Donthar in the midsection and knocked him back a few paces. Wind whipped off Argantyr's blade, but Donthar caught the blow on his axe handle, more splinters flying. Argantyr closed in, and the two of them stood straining, broadsword and battle-axe locked together momentarily, legs braced and pushing the two warriors into one another, steel on steel. Argantyr grunted and pushed Donthar's axe back a few inches towards the warrior. Then, a few more inches.

"Now, Executioner, you don't face a helpless girl in steel manacles for you to torture at your leisure! You face King Argantyr Fenris! Know that her name was Friona, and I loved her! That is why I am going to kill you; then the Giant!"

Argantyr could see Donthar's eyes go wide inside of his hood, then Argantyr ripped the hood from Donthar's head revealing a face disfigured by chemicals and war. Argantyr head-butted Donthar, and the man fell sitting on the floor, blood streaming down his face. But even with his vision obscured by a broken nose, the Executioner was a dangerous man. No sooner had Donthar hit the floor than he was swinging his mighty axe-blade at Argantyr's legs. Argantyr leapt high and came down with a blow from his broadsword that split Donthar's head like a melon. Bits of skull flew up and pelted back down, and brain matter seeped out onto the floor of Thannhausefeer's great hall.

Argantyr's ears rung, and his head throbbed from the head-butt he had delivered to Donthar. The memories burst through his brain like water from a broken dam.

Thannhausefeer overturned the massive table to his feasting hall and bellowed. The chamber rumbled as if it were in an earthquake.

"Aye! The jig is up, Giant! You know why I am here, and I know that you didn't plan on anyone leaving the Isle of Bones with any of your treasure!" Argantyr shouted, plucking the dagger from the belt at his hip and throwing it into Thannhausefeer's left eye. The Giant roared with pain.

Argantyr clutched his wolf-hooded head in agony. "I remember! Damn you, Giant! I remember! Freae Nome gonastre! Kreedolph hgnome Fenrir! Krynestrees Ryedorf! Hoathehe Fenrir!" Argantyr shouted and fell to one knee as the transformation began. His face contorted and stretched. His clothes ripped, and he instantly expanded in size, silver hair sprouting from his skin. An elongated snout burst from his face, opening wide a mouthful of deadly razor-like fangs.

Thannhausefeer had managed to pluck the dagger from his eye. He picked up his throne and threw it at the werewolf, but the creature had already moved from its spot and passed by the Giant, ripping a chunk out of his inner thigh with its deadly fangs. Thannhausefeer's knee buckled. He stumbled backwards and reached for the enormous broadsword on the wall. The werewolf lunged at the Giant. It stood nearly as tall as Thannhausefeer on its hind legs. The beast locked powerful jaws on the Giant's face and Thanhausefeer clumsily dropped his sword as Giant and werewolf tumbled across the floor.

Blood filled Thannhausefeer's eyes from his savaged face, and he could no longer see. He felt along the beast's fur for its throat and clutched at empty air.

"You've blinded me! Damn you!" The Giant felt for his table to brace himself. Trying to stand, his face gored, and his right eye hanging from its socket, the Giant fell, slumping to the floor.

Thannhausefeer heard the padding of feet coming down the hall towards his chamber. He heard the heavy breathing of the beast within the great hall and an almost human sound of laughter coming from the werewolf. It sounded like the sawing of wood.

"No! Lydiana! Stay away!" Thannhausefeer shouted.

The Giant's daughter screamed. It was too late. The monstrous supernatural wolf gripped Lydiana in its powerful jaws and slung her like a rag doll. She crashed into the wall, and there was a thump and the snapping of bones. She screamed again. The werewolf locked his jaws on the woman and slung her a second time; another thump—and more bones crunched.

The creature dragged her over beside of her father. Lydiana was unable to move and lay gasping for air but still conscious. Raising himself up on one arm and mustering his strength, Thannhausefeer grasped his enormous broadsword and swung it single-handedly where he heard the werewolf laughing, but the blade cut empty air; then the beast had its front paws on Thannhausefeer's chest, tearing the Giant's throat out. Lydiana could hear Thannhausefeer's screams segueing into gurgling as blood frothed from his mouth and ran onto the chamber floor. The werewolf quickly slung Lydiana out of the way so she would not drown in the blood gushing from the dying Giant's mouth.

---

Argantyr rocked on all fours, clad only in the giant silver wolf skin. Crimson flowing from the dead Giant's blood matted Argantyr's dark hair and beard, streaming down his naked chest and torso.

Armies had fallen before Argantyr and his hosts, and the ending was always the same. The pain of the man becoming the beast and becoming the man again. *Why should it be any different this time?*

The wounds sustained in the fight with Donthar were quickly healing; the transformation from man to wolf and back to man always insured a quick recovery in the aftermath of battle.

He clutched at his stomach and retched up blood and bits of the giant's flesh. While the beast enjoyed consuming the blood of his enemies, the man had little taste for it. It had been the price of empire.

Once the effects of transformation back to a man had subsided, Argantyr rummaged the antechambers of Thannhausefeer's castle and managed to find enough dead warriors' garments and furs that hadn't yet been disposed of. Some of them were an ill fit, but Argantyr made the best of a bad situation. He had done it before. Generally, he prepared before a battle with a fresh change of clothes; but this time circumstances hadn't allowed for it.

Argantyr could hear the woman's heavy breathing. He went over and knelt down beside her.

"Manannan, I didn't want you to die. I wanted to sail away with you, but I knew he wouldn't let me go. He kept me here as… as a memento of my mother." She gasped, sucking in air.

Argantyr knew that Lydiana had probably thought about running away with him, but he also knew that she had enough of the cruel Giant's blood in her that she enjoyed the suffering of others.

Argantyr cradled Lydiana's head in his left hand so she could see him as he spoke to her. "Listen, woman, my name is Argantyr. That dead woman whose skin you danced in belonged to King Friodere's daughter, Friona. I loved her." With his last words, Argantyr slammed his dagger down into Lydiana's chest. The blow made a thumping sound like a melon struck by a hammer, and blood jettisoned up from the quietus. The woman strangled on the blood frothing from her mouth. Her rheumy eyes widened as she looked upon the House of Shades; and then Lydiana expired.

With his sword slung over his back and his dagger at his hip, he listened for movement amidst the silence of Thannhausefeer's castle. His wolfen senses were still strong and warned him of no impending danger, but he left his scabbard tip untied. It always paid to be cautious.

*They must have hidden themselves away after hearing what went on in the great hall. It is just as well. I long to be free of the madness of Thannhausefeer's castle and leave this Isle of Bones.*

---

Argantyr paced the smoky snow covered shore as he looked upon the burning ships crumbling to ashes. Thannhausefeer had set fire to them all.

A ghostly figure appeared on down the shore, barely in his line of vision under the dim sunless sky. The stinging winter wind whipped the woman's billowing white gown and blonde hair. He couldn't make out the features of her face from such a distance with the biting wind blurring his vision. He followed her on down the shore for a while but never seemed to gain any distance on her. She raised her arm languorously and pointed to a ship sailing just on the horizon. By the red and white striped sail with the banner of the great bird of prey in the center, Argantyr knew that it was one of King Friodere's Sea Hawks, and therefore friendly.

"Ho! Sea Hawk! It is Argantyr Fenris! Ho!" he called to the crew of the ship.

Argantyr could see them lowering a lifeboat and men filing in it to row ashore. Though he surmised that reason had told King Friodere that his daughter was probably dead by now, Argantyr knew there was still hope in his friend's heart. He dreaded breaking the news to the old king. If Friodere had only summoned Argantyr to look for her sooner…

While he waited for the rescue boat Argantyr scanned the shore for the Woman in White, but there was no sign of her.

# FULL MOON REVENANT

Six-year-old Donal Feogh tossed and turned in his tiny, hay-filled bed. The full moon cast its rays down on him through the window of the cottage on the edge of the forest. A lone wolf howled in the distance. No other animals made a sound, and the great grey autumn forest—thick with birch and hazel, hawthorn and ash—basked in moonbeam and desolation.

The constant rattling of Donal's wooden-framed bed kept his mother and sister awake. His father snored in drunken slumber, and Donal's mother knew if her husband woke up, the whole family would pay for the disturbance.

"Klissa!" Mollae Feogh called in a loud whisper to the young woman lying in her hay bed across the room.

"Yes, Mother?"

"Go to the barn and be quiet about it. Milk ol' Bess and bring it back here for Donal. The night milk will settle him in, so we can all get some sleep."

Klissa took a bucket and quietly slipped through the front door of the moss-grown house. The barn was set a few hundred feet from the dwelling. The baying of the lone wolf cut the stillness of night like a sword of steel. There was something in the wolf's howl that was unnatural. The young woman's heart quickened.

When Klissa arrived at Bess's stall, the cow was in turmoil. The bovine was twisting and turning, walking back and forth; she wouldn't be still.

"Shh. Shh," Klissa told the animal, but Bess was fit to be tied.

Klissa raised the latch on the door and walked into the barn stall with Bess. When Klissa was inside the stall and the latch holding the door clicked into place, she heard something huge crash through the thicket in front of her family's house. A bestial growl accompanied the noise as the door to her family's house crashed in.

Klissa ran for the doorway of the barn and stopped dead in her tracks. By the light of the full and argent moon she could see the figure entering her home. It was the largest wolf she had ever seen. The thing stood on its hind legs like a man, at least seven feet tall. The monster snarled.

Klissa backed up into the shadows of the barn and pressed herself into a corner. She could hear her mother screaming and gurgling as her throat was being torn out. Her little brother cried in agony as the beast ripped him apart like a rag doll.

Klissa wanted to help them, but what could she do against an enormous creature of such ferocity? She chanced a glimpse at the house from inside the barn door. Her father came tumbling outside through the door of their home. Sobered by the sudden deaths of his wife and son, the former soldier gripped his sword. He slashed and hacked at the creature wildly, but to no avail. He might as well have tried to cut solid iron.

Klissa's father gave ground as the giant supernatural wolf paced leisurely forward, enduring her father's futile sword strokes. The creature made a sound like the sawing of wood. It looked to be laughing at her father, toying with him.

The beast threw its forelimbs up in the air, all but saying, *Do your best, hairless weakling*!

Klissa's father took the opportunity to shove cold steel through the beast's guts. The werewolf stood silent for a moment, its malevolent eyes gleaming with uncanny intelligence. Gripping the sword with its hairy claws, the beast tore the blade from its stomach and roared so loud it sounded as if it was inside the barn with Klissa.

The werewolf slashed a claw across her father's face, and the man hit the ground. The beast didn't wait for him to rise. It picked him up and followed up with another slash across the man's gored face. The monster raised Klissa's father off the ground with one claw and held him by the neck. He dangled like a doll at a puppet show Klissa had seen in the village. The werewolf's movement was a blur as it shoved its other claw through Klissa's father's chest and pulled out the man's heart. It made a sound like a boot splashing through wet mud and coming free.

The werewolf threw his head back and bayed to the glowing orb in the sky. He sniffed the air, and his head turned slowly towards the barn where Klissa hoped to remain undetected. Klissa flattened herself against the barn wall and swallowed hard. She heard the beast galloping on all fours.

Suddenly its cold snout was touching her nose and lightly nuzzling her flaxen hair. How had it gotten there so quickly? A low growl came from the monster, and its claw shot up to grasp her by the throat. Klissa could feel blood trickling down her breasts. The beast sniffed, savoring the aroma of her blood commingling with her womanhood. It pressed Klissa's head against the boards of the barn and inserted its manhood into her. Klissa screamed. The creature slammed Klissa into the side of the barn over and over while she continued to scream. Her blood was running down her legs. The monster grunted as it violated her. Klissa's eyes rolled back in her head and life left her desecrated shell. The werewolf continued to thrust fervently into her some moments after she had expired.

"And we were surrounded on one side by Sarssenians and on the other by Aniochans. Two hereditary enemies that sacrificed to the same sandy god!" Berico's voice rang through the antechamber. The ruddy-faced one-eye paused to quaff ale from his foaming jack and continued. "Fortunate for us the damned snake-men stayed out of what they had started in the first place. Always them behind it!" He paused for another drink.

"So both tribes have us surrounded, and we are trying to secure the eastern borders. Tell everyone who wasn't there might as well tell us who were there too—how we got out of that one with our hides intact," Thalric said. The warrior endeavored to stop Berico's narrative from deteriorating into a tirade about the politics of the turbulent East, where Sarssenia encroached on the west and would ultimately try to invade Tuatha. All of Berico's conversations eventually led there.

Berico swigged more ale and his thumb jerked in Argantyr's direction. King Argantyr Faoladh lolled in his big oaken chair, a smile forming at the corners of his mouth. His piercing green eyes blazed in his battle-scarred face, and his long black beard hung down the front of his sleeveless silk shirt. His hair fell down over broad shoulders onto his animal hide vest. Argantyr brought up his drinking jack and sipped. Steel sinews rippled, and his movements were as fluid as a panther's. Behind Argantyr's chair hung a giant silver wolf skin on a rack fastened to the stone wall. Beside the huge pelt was a gleaming broadsword with a night-black pattern weaving sinuously through the blade, shining like liquid onyx.

Across from Argantyr sat Thalric. Next to the blond-haired, blue-eyed captain of the guard sat his newly appointed general, Thaesius. Thaesius stood well over six feet, and knotty muscles rippled beneath his sun-darkened skin. The man had an aquiline nose, and his swarthy face was framed by curly, shoulder-length hair. His piercing dark eyes dilated as he listened to the drunken Berico continue his tale.

"Usually Argantyr waits to see how the battle goes," he spewed. "But this time he turns to me and Thalric and says, 'No way out but to fight to the death. There will be no prisoners taken on either side.' And before those sand maggots knew what hit 'em, Argantyr leapt from his mount and was runnin' among them as the wolf, shreddin' their throats and tearin' beatin' hearts from mailed chests. I was takin' down two at a time—sword in one hand, mace in the other–crushin' skulls and spillin' innards like I was bein' paid by the head. Thalric was mowin' down sand-maggots like chaff before a scythe, and I seen one sneakin' around his back with a dagger. This was back when I had two good eyes and…"

Thalric interrupted in his stoic Northern accent. "You've had an eye missing ever since you were a boy, you filthy dog. By the time someone told you you would go blind if you kept interfering with yourself, you had already lost one eye."

The half-dozen warriors sitting around Argantyr's table roared with laughter. The men swilled more ale, and when the laughter died down, the conversation in the Wolf's Lair took a more somber turn.

Argantyr's advisor, Talus, spoke. "The people grow more fearful by the day with talk of the werewolf, Argantyr. Especially after what happened to that girl last night."

Argantyr fixed his burning emerald gaze on Talus. "Go on. What do they say?"

Talus nodded his head, knowing what Argantyr expected. "It isn't popular opinion yet, but, of course, some say their own king slaughters them in their beds on a night of a full moon. There have been two nights of carnage thus far and several killings on each of those nights."

Argantyr's eyes swept around the table, studying every face in the room. "Of course," he said, calmly taking a pull from his drinking jack.

Berico broke the silence. "Damned fools don't remember a time when the whole of Tuath was in the grip of that tyrant Seanchai and his black wizard Nog-Zaygar. Not only did Argantyr have to put down a whole country of puppet rulers, but he nearly lost his life fightin' Seanchai and his magician. But in the end the two of them's heads was on spears in front of this castle, and Argantyr was sittin' on that throne out there." Berico pointed to the door of the antechamber leading out into Argantyr's great hall. "Now the people don't have to go about in fear of their women bein' outraged at a soldier's whim or they themselves being dragged off to Seanchai's torture chambers, never to return."

"Yes. They forget," Argantyr said. He looked studiously at the faces of those seated around the table and added, "But not everyone forgets." He hinted at something cryptic and ominous, and all was silent again.

Thalric's words were as an assassin's dagger piercing the stillness of the little chamber where the men were gathered. "I suppose most of them don't understand that Argantyr can change into the werewolf anytime he chooses with the wolf skin. He doesn't have to wait until the full of the moon. But maybe it is better they only know superstitions and not the methods of the black arts. It helps to keep fools from dreaming of conquest."

"We hunt tonight!" Argantyr rumbled, taking a pull from his cup.

"But last night the moon was full. If our murderer can only become a lycanthrope under the full moon, what can we hope to find tonight?" Talus asked.

"Tonight the werewolf will show himself... one way or the other,"

## THE SNAKE-MAN'S BANE

Argantyr replied.

These men knew Argantyr understood things other men dared not fathom. They would have followed him into Hel if that is where he led. No one disputed his word. Argantyr held up his drinking jack and said, "To the hunt!" He downed the remainder of his ale, and his men followed suit.

Argantyr got up and removed his vest, taking the wolf skin from its hanger. He flung the great pelt about his shoulders and fastened it. While the others went to don their armor, Argantyr took the scabbarded sword from his waist and traded it for the blade with the swirling pattern of jet on the wall.

---

The dim autumn sun was setting on the mountains surrounding the castle of Ta-Rah—the hill from which the High King, Argantyr Faoladh, ruled over all of the Tuathic states. Argantyr led the hunting party of half a dozen warriors toward the forest where only last night the girl's family had been slaughtered and she herself violated unto death.

The last rays of the sun glinted on burnished helmets, silver breastplates, and gilt-worked mail. The men were armed with swords and battle-axes. The hooves of their warhorses clopped and crunched dried twigs and brittle, fallen leaves as they entered the Meathian forest.

They rode their mounts to a point where a path was worn through the trees. The warriors followed the road until it branched off in two directions. Argantyr threw up his gauntleted arm, signaling the small band to stop. Looking straight ahead, he told them, "Thalric, you and Berico lead the men to the house where that girl and her family were slaughtered last night. Thaesius will ride with me back to Ta-Rah. If you don't find our killer, beat it back to the castle. I think the werewolf will be showing himself soon."

Argantyr turned his head and looked at Thalric, squinting. Thalric nodded his head ever so slightly, letting Argantyr know he was aware that the king knew something the rest of them didn't.

Without another word Thalric led the men down the fork veering off to the right. It would come out into dense forest less than a mile from where last night's murders had occurred.

Argantyr sat motionless on his mount until the warriors were out of sight. As the last horse disappeared through the trees, he looked at Thaesius and motioned with his head in the direction back to the castle. Argantyr gripped the reins of his steed and began leading him back the way they had come. Thaesius put a reed to his mouth and blew. The dart hissed through the air. Argantyr heard the sibilant missile too late. The dart drove into the back of his neck. He spun his horse to face Thaesius, hand clutching at his half-drawn sword as he toppled from his horse and hit the ground. Thaesius ambled his mount over to where Argantyr lay and grinned down sardonically at the fallen king.

---

Thaesius's vulturine countenance slowly came into view as Argantyr regained consciousness. Torches set in sconces illuminated the chamber. Inside the spacious cavern, massive stalactites hung down like the teeth of mythical beasts. Thaesius sat on a natural rock formation jutting up from the ground. He was wearing Argantyr's wolf cloak.

"For a man so great as to have carved a kingdom out of half of the western world, you surprise me with your recklessness, Argantyr."

Argantyr felt no constriction from any physical bonds, but try as he might, he could do no more than blink his eyes and swallow.

"That's right. You can't move. Tying you up was unnecessary. My dart was soaked in ju-ju grisha—a plant used by the Boccu mud-men in the dark jungles of Tocar-Kuhl to temporarily paralyze their foes. I know you have ranged far and might even know what that is. But don't worry, I'm not going to make you into a *xulla* to mindlessly serve me as the mud-men's priests do their own kind. You aren't going to live that long."

Argantyr tried rolling his tongue to form words. All that escaped his throat was a grunt.

"Ha ha! You still can't talk. I know. This isn't the first time I have used the ju-ju darts. So, you will let me talk for a while and you will listen, aye, Argantyr?"

The sinister grin faded from Thaesius's face and after a short pause he waxed somber. "A long time ago there was a boy named Kelakon, son of the Aegolian emperor, Ajaxian. When Ajaxian died, Kelakon ascended the throne…"

Argantyr growled in a low voice, "And we both know how your father died, kinslayer. I knew you the moment I set eyes on you, you son of a bitch!"

Thaesius turned his head to the side and looked at Argantyr incredulously. "Your voice has returned quicker than I expected, Argantyr. It must be the years of going forth on all fours has changed you as a man. It certainly has me. No matter. Allow me to continue. Where was I?"

"You were going to tell how you killed your father, Kelakon. About how your tyrannical rule saw men and women stripped of their dignity on a daily basis by your rapine and torture. You crushed your own people like insects beneath your heel. Your own sister wasn't even safe from your lecherousness…"

"Enough!" Kelakon shouted. "You are one to talk, usurper. Leading mercenaries into civilized kingdoms and running on the ground as a beast. Ripping and rending while your men take whatever they want. Lining your coffers with more gold and jewels with each empire that crumpled in the iron fist of Argantyr Faoladh!" Kelakon roared, his voice reverberating through the cave. But you made me, Argantyr! You made me what I am now!"

"I thought I killed you, Kelakon. I seem to remember your blood on my sword. But here you are."

"You insult me, Argantyr. You can't even remember how you killed, Kelakon? Am I that insignificant to you? Has Argantyr slain so many kings that he can't count them?"

Argantyr tried to nod his head, but he still couldn't move.

"You had me on the ground savaging my face. Your wolf's muzzle reaching for my throat. But then, Argantyr, the hero, caught a glimpse out of the corner of his eye. One of your warriors was surrounded on all sides by my Marmidian guard, and Argantyr the wolf charged in to tear their flesh to shreds. I lay unconscious and forgotten on the battlefield. To fight another day. Today is that day!" Kelakon tightened his lips and raised his head, sneering down at Argantyr.

"I was badly scarred, but I lived. Though I had never known what it meant to live until the first full moon after that battle. Then the change came upon me. When I changed to a man again, the scars were gone. I had never felt stronger. Of course you don't need me to tell you. You know all too well. You made me what I am. But once every full moon is not enough for me. That is why I am wearing your cloak. I wanted you to know this before you die, Argantyr. I always felt that Ajaxian—the man who inseminated my mother—was much too altruistic and weak to govern Aegolia. He had to die so that a stronger man could give such a splendid kingdom the ruler it deserved. No, Ajaxian was not my father. You are. He merely made my birth possible. But you gave me life! You aren't weak like Ajaxian was, but you are still a fool!"

Argantyr's fingertips twitched, and he burst out laughing. "You calling another man a fool is quite the jest, Kelakon. You do realize that my cloak you now wear is as useless as any mangy old hide without the proper invocation?"

"You mean such as the one written in that musty tome, *On the Black Art of the Fenrir* and *Becoming the Lycanthrope*?" Kelakon paused, giving Argantyr time to realize the severity of his situation. "I was a scholar even before I was a king, Argantyr. Or did you think you were the only man who could both wield a sword and read?" Kelakon chuckled mockingly.

"I know that you are trying to stall for time, Argantyr. You are probably hoping your men will find you before I can kill you. I also know that you are regaining the use of your limbs and soon will be able to swing a sword. I am no fool. I may or may not be a match for you, steel on steel, but that is not what I have in mind. No, I plan to give you the same opportunity you gave me—man against beast, cold steel against the dark powers drawn down from the outer gulfs. Powers I intend to use to reclaim my kingdom and then some. Feel your sword at your side. Look at it. I didn't take it. I intend for you to use it for what good it does you. You didn't even bring a silver sword to hunt a werewolf." Kelakon sneered.

"If you would have been a little more thorough in your reading, Kelakon, you would have realized that silver swords are a poor choice against lycanthropy."

But Argantyr's words fell on deaf ears as Kelakon sonorously intoned the barbaric words ringing throughout the cavern: "Freae Nome gonastre! Kreedolph hgnome Fenrir! Krynestrees Ryedorf! Hoathehe Fenrir!"

Kelakon took a step back, bracing his right leg against the pain, both hands clutching his head. He wasn't used to changing as fast as Argantyr, but still the transformation of man to beast was coming on quickly. Kelakon's face stretched into an elongated snout, and silver hair sprouted all over his body. He opened his mouth and slavered through dirk-like fangs.

Argantyr pumped his fists and flexed his arms in an effort to get blood moving through them. He tried to stand and fell.

Kelakon screamed in agony as his spine crackled, and black claws now appeared where his hands had been. He climbed in stature to well over seven feet. The werewolf lunged at Argantyr as he managed to get to his feet. His sword whistled from scabbard and slashed the werewolf's side, raking its ribs. Blood trailed the blade and splattered the floor of the great cavern. The beast looked down at its wound and then looked at Argantyr.

"What I started to tell you before you interrupted me is a silver sword isn't worth much for dispatching a lycanthrope to the House of Shades. But this, boy. This is death!" Argantyr's face was a demonic mask as he thumbed the silver blade swirled with pitch-black enigma.

The werewolf circled Argantyr slowly, understanding in its cruel eyes. Argantyr stepped forward into a fighting stance and swung the broadsword again. The werewolf's claw shot out in an effort to wrench the weapon from Argantyr's hand, but instead the monster pulled back a stump and its blood jetted freely. The beast's claw lay twitching on the floor of the cave.

Voices of men and the clopping of horses' hooves could be heard in

## THE SNAKE-MAN'S BANE

the distance. The beast turned to run from the cave. Argantyr leapt onto the rocky formation where Kelakon had sat earlier and jumped back off, driving the sword into the werewolf's back. The blade went through the monster's heart and came out the front of his chest. Argantyr gritted his teeth. Rivulets of sweat stung his eyes. He continued to put his weight on the blade until the beast's death throes subsided.

"Argantyr?" Thalric shouted. "Are you in there?"

"Ho, Thalric!" Breathing heavily, Argantyr shouted as loud as he could. "I am here."

Argantyr could see Berico and Thalric's faces illuminated by the torches blazing along the cavern walls.

"He's back here, you dogs!" Berico called to the others.

"We saw your horse, and you weren't on it, so we knew you'd found the werewolf. We followed your mount here to the cave mouth, but he refused to enter. He's taken quite a liking to you, but not that much of a liking." Berico said.

"Where is Thaesius?" asked Thalric.

Argantyr nodded his head at the werewolf. The beast shrunk and reverted back to the man lying dead on the cavern floor.

Berico whistled in astonishment. "Well, it looks like you got him."

Argantyr nodded and pulled the sword from Kelakon's corpse and quickly removed his bloody cloak from his enemy's dead body.

He held up the cloak and examined it. "The hole has already closed up. It just needs to be cleaned."

The men stood staring at Thaesius until Argantyr broke the silence. "He told us he was Thaesius, but I knew him as Kelakon from the past. I remembered killing him at the battle of Aegolia ten years ago, or so I thought. Still, my memory is good and I knew him to be the kinslayer and usurper whom I slew, or a twin. That day on the battlefield the change was upon me and I attacked Kelakon, but I was called away—more likely than not to save one of your hides—and I left him be. The attack caused him to change, but only when the moon rose full, since he had no cloak to control it."

"The sword…" Thalric nodded at the blade Argantyr held, covered in blood and dripping onto the igneous floor. "It doesn't appear to be made of silver. But the black metal swirling through the blade… if it is indeed metal at all…"

"Silver swords are of little use against a lycanthrope. They are too brittle to hold up and not very effective, even if by some miracle they aren't shattered. It is superstition. If it wasn't, I would have been dead a long time ago."

Argantyr patted the sword hanging at his side. "No, the witch,

Bunduica gave me the precious metal—if you want to call it that—as a gift. It comes from another world named Hahg-Klaath. The witch showed me Hahg-Klaath in a crystal prism. The prism shifted angles as I looked into it. Inside the prism, standing by a river under a black sun were robed figures with eyes glowing like burning coals. The figures lining the river's edge chanted in unison, and the river roared as though it were a living beast. The riverbed flowed with the substance you see swirling through my blade.

"I felt a sense of drunkenness, like my head was being turned upside down on my shoulders and my limbs were exchanging positions. That is when Bunduica warned me away from the prism and covered it with a voluminous sable veil. She said it was only safe to look into it for a moment. Any longer, and I was in danger of letting the entities that haunted Hahg-Klaath into our own world. They worked frantically at unlocking the ever-shifting angles of the prism and could quickly make their way here. Such is the way of a sorceress, to ever court disaster.

"She said her demon lover, Thorn, brought back the substance from Hahg-Klaath that makes the sword lethal to lycanthropes. No matter; the witch's demon lover gave me specific instructions as to the construction of the sword to pass on to the blacksmith who forged the blade. Baldric, the best smith in all of Skaldavia, made the sword."

Argantyr whipped the blade from his scabbard and handed it to Thalric to examine. All of the men gathered around to look closely at the werewolf's bane. Thalric inspected the blade and with an approving grunt returned the sword to Argantyr, who sheathed it in its scabbard.

"Let's beat it back to the Wolf's Lair for a foaming jack or ten. Killing is thirsty work," Argantyr said.

"Aye," Berico grunted.

"Aye," The rest of the men joined in in agreement.

Without another word, the warriors all turned to go. And they left he who had lived his life as a wicked beast to rot in desolation on the floor of that abandoned cave.

Printed in Great Britain
by Amazon